Presented with Love

Tara Kennedy

Table of Contents

About This Story

Helena's plans for the weekend involved going to the Hawaiian Expo in Las Vegas, and hanging out with her grandmother. But when a flight snafu puts her in the airport hotel bar next to a hot guy, she takes full advantage. But the guy disappears on her. And when she gets to Vegas it turns out her tutu has signed her up for a televised competition based on a Christmas song, and one of the other contestants is that guy who ghosted her? Helena's competitive spirit kicks into gear.

Makoa is good at hockey, it's off-ice where he seems to fumble. So when he finds his mom has signed him up for a TV show, well, he's hoping for a Christmas miracle. Because Helena is rightfully annoyed at him, and he needs to stay in the competition long enough to prove he's worth another chance. Otherwise this will be his last day of Christmas.

Copyright

To Grandma Eva, who loved romances, and also had to share a birthday with Christmas.

Chapter 1

Helena Alaka'i Smith had let her coworker Miles handle the travel arrangements for the conference, even though they needed separate flights back, and now she was paying for it. Luckily for Miles his plane had departed with him on it an hour ago.

"Okay," Helena said to the kind but confused airline agent. "So my reservation is just a reservation but not an actual ticket. So what do we need to do to make it a ticket?" Helena was headed to Las Vegas, for the Hawaiian Expo and- more importantly - some good relaxation time with her tutu. If Miles made her miss seeing her grandmother, well, Helena wasn't quite sure how she would get him, but somehow, she would.

"I'm not sure," said Jenna. "I can pull up the number, but it no longer had your information attached to it, so I can't tell."

"Okay, can you attach a ticket to Vegas to that number?" Helena asked sweetly. She loved solving bureaucratic problems, but after four days of high energy conferencing, she wanted to be on her way to Vegas where there was a pool. And fun. Work conferencing was fun, but in a staid work way.

"Um, let me try."

Helena kept her smile bright, though she could tell from the clock that there was no way she was getting on her scheduled flight. Or reserved but not actually scheduled flight. She didn't want to warn her grandmother until they had a backup plan in place. Tutu was pretty easy breezy about plans, but due to various issues Helena hadn't seen her in two years, and she needed to see her. Almost as much as she needed to veg at a pool.

Eventually, with the help up Helena's credit card just in case, Jenna got Helena booked, not just reserved, on a flight to Vegas the following morning. "There's one more flight tonight, that you can try to fly standby on. But it goes through Dallas. It's storming there, so it's already been delayed. And our standby list already has 20 people on it, so I don't think the odds are good. But I can add you."

"Tomorrow's is direct?" Helena asked. She pulled up hotels that accepted the points on her card near the airport. She had been hoping to use these points for something cooler than this. But hey.

"It is."

"I'll stick with that. Thanks, Jenna. I appreciate everything." Helena smiled and took her bag back off the scale and made her way to where the hotel advised that there would be a shuttle. She set an alarm for 3 am, because she was going to be at that airport well before her 6am flight to account for any further weirdness. Her phone buzzed with a confirmation email. Comparing it to the original one Miles had sent her, she could see differences now. She was going to kill him once she was back in DC with him.

Helena got checked in at the hotel then picked up her phone. "Hey, Tutu, small change in plans."

"Helena Alaka'i, what is small? Aren't you on a plane right now? Wait, are you calling from the plane?"

"I am not calling from the plane. There was an issue with my reservation, and so I couldn't get on the plane. But they have rebooked me onto a flight very early tomorrow, so I will be there in time for breakfast. I promise." Helena knocked on the wooden headboard. But seriously, she better be there in time for breakfast.

"Oh, okay. I will miss having dinner with you tonight. I guess I will need to call my friend Lois and see what she is up to."

"I hope you all have the best dinner. I'm sorry I won't be there to join you, but breakfast is on me tomorrow."

"The hotel gives us breakfast."

"Well, then I can afford to be generous," Helena said.

"Oh you," Tutu said. "Okay, I probably won't be up when you leave tomorrow, but text me that you are on the plane so I don't worry. And have you eaten dinner?"

"Not yet, but that's next on my list." The one very tiny silver lining was not having to eat on the plane. Or drink. Because Helena had definitely earned a cocktail.

MAKOA WILSON WAS GREAT on skates, nimble, able to react on the fly. On land where he sometimes struggled. He thought he had accounted for everything. He was meeting his family in Las Vegas for the Hawaiian Expo. His car had started making noises, so - no problem. He dropped the car off at the mechanic, and took a taxi to the airport.

The weather in Denver was crisp and clear, perfect flying weather. Apparently it was the weather in Dallas that had cancelled the first leg of his flight. So now he had a new plan. He just needed to call his mom and tell her. He found a quiet corner, took a deep breath. Makoa did not like disappointing his mom. He had missed a few flights home due to his own failure to plan, hut hopefully his mom would agree the weather was outside of his control. "Hi, Mom, there was a storm in Dallas so I'm going to be arriving early tomorrow instead."

"Makoa, if I type in the weather in Dallas will there really be a storm or did you oversleep again?"

"Mom, I promise there was a storm in Dallas." Makoa had only ever missed his flight due to oversleeping - okay like seven times. The hockey team assistant manager now had a key to his apartment to come rouse him if needed. And well, early morning tomorrow was a risk, but he just figured he wouldn't go to sleep tonight. Can't oversleep if you never sleep. It was a foolproof plan.

"Okay, Muli Hope, we will see you tomorrow. You know how to get to the hotel? Do you have the address?"

"Yes, I have all that info," Makoa said patiently.

"Okay, we'll see you tomorrow. Your sisters and I are going out to dinner. Make sure you eat."

"Yes, I am going to eat." Makoa was ravenous. He had not snacked before arriving at the airport. Now he needed enough food to make up for that. And to keep the drinks he planned to consume in the airport hotel bar tonight company.

He loved his family, but he was always the muli hope, the youngest child, even though his sisters now had kids of their own. And well, he was not in control of the weather. He hadn't been able to find a direct flight that didn't leave butt early in the morning. He should have picked an earlier flight to give himself more cushion. He was also trying to make it to as many off season workouts as he could, trying to be the guy who put in all the work.

But now here he was having booked a hotel room, because tall brown dudes lurking in airports were considered suspicious. And he wanted food that was not from the airport. Airport hotel food was almost as expensive, but you could eat it in a chair, while your luggage stayed upstairs. His apartment was about two hours away. Once he got home, he'd only have an hour or two before he needed to be on the way back. So the airport hotel seemed simpler, if a bit more expensive.

The minor league hockey salary wasn't huge, but he usually didn't splurge much, and he was sure that this year he'd get picked to go up a slot. He'd been a great prospect coming out of college. Not flashy, but solid. He knew the flashy guys would get picked to go up first, and he was okay with that. But now it was his turn. Had to be.

But for today he was gonna go down and get dinner. He set like six alarms on his phone and asked for a wakeup call from the front desk. But a drink, some dinner, and then a ton of coffee, and he'd be good.

"Sir," the hostess at the hotel restaurant said, "would you mind sitting at the bar? We've got a big family coming down, they were on their way to a wedding, and they are taking up most of our tables."

"Oh, that's fine," Makoa said. "As long as I can get food."

"Of course."

At the bar, he took an open stool and scanned the menu the hostess had given him. He made an order with the bartender. "After the drink I'm going to need to switch to coffee for an early flight. In fact, I might just park myself here until then."

The bartender nodded. "No problem. Though we close up around two."

"That's perfect actually," Makoa said.

"How early is your flight?" the woman two stools down asked. She wore a dress that hugged her curves and had long wavy dark hair.

"Six," Makoa said.

"Mine's six-thirty. I guess that's why my plan was to catnap. But I applaud your spirit."

"I have been known to oversleep. And my first flight got pushed because of the storm. If I miss this, my family will never let me live it down."

"Ah, family. I'm on my way to see my grandmother, who well, she's my favorite part of my family, ssh, don't tell. I don't get to see her enough."

Makoa's grandparents lived in Hawai'i so he understood not getting to see them enough. They were traveling less these days, so had opted not to come to Vegas for the Hawaiian expo.

The hostess brought another person to the bar, and he looked at the stool between Makoa and the woman. "Do you all want to sit together?"

"Sure," the woman said, sliding her cocktail, and then herself down one. "Thanks," she said to the other man.

He nodded and waved over the bartender.

"So," she said, "I'm Helena by the way."

Chapter 2

"**I**'m Makoa," the guy said.

The polo shirt and chinos he wore seemed a little stuffy, but if he was planning to see family, that explained it. Helena often wore yoga pants on trips. But she had broken out a dress with leggings, so that her grandmother didn't ask her if they needed to hurry to make it to her yoga class when she arrived at the hotel. Tutu loved comfortable clothing, but she had not embraced the athleisure wear trend.

"So, do you live in Colorado, or just passing through?" Helena asked.

The bartender dropped her pasta dish in front of her. She nodded her thanks. She was so hungry.

"I live in Colorado. How familiar are you with the area?"

"I was just in town for a work conference. So basically, I have seen downtown Denver."

"Ah, so I live not in downtown Denver. I'm in a suburb, so about an hour and a half - like 60 miles away."

"Wow, I live in DC, and I think you'd have to leave in the dead of night to get 60 miles in an hour."

"Oh DC, that seems like a cool place."

"I agree, but that is not always the reaction I get from people," Helena said. She had learned to work it in early when traveling. If people were gonna be weird about it, she needed to know that upfront. It wasn't always a deal breaker. Sometimes just a sign that some people weren't going to get any hotter with further conversation - so they should move on to the next phase of the evening.

"Well, I like places that have hockey teams."

"Are you into hockey?"

"You could say that," Makoa said. "How about you?"

"I like hockey. Although I confess, I never really bought into the whole have to support a team just because of geography. That seems super limiting."

"Interesting. It used to be much harder to watch any other teams, but now with like the hockey package and the internet, you can keep track of so many more teams. Though I guess, your local stadium probably hopes you'll come buy tickets."

"I've been a few times. It's a fun thing."

"So do you have a favorite team or you are more equal opportunity?"

"I tend to pick the team wearing the most interesting colors."

"Which, since the home teams wear the white jerseys, probably means you end up picking the away teams."

"Sometimes. I also sometimes like the cooler names. Washington is the Domes, which you have to admit is very dull."

"I like their colors though. But I admit buildings are less interesting than animals or weather events. DC has a minor league team, but they play a little farther away. Pennsylvania, I think. They are animals."

"Okay, I actually didn't know there was a minor league. But okay."

"Yeah. Whole second league with tournaments and everything."

"Huh. Makes sense, I guess. Can't rely on college alone."

"Anyway, it's the offseason. So, what do you do for work?"

Helena liked that he kept turning the questions around, seeming as interested in getting to know her as in talking about himself. "Oh, I work for a professional association. It's not very interesting. It only seems interesting once a year when they send me to the annual conference."

"Okay, what do you do with your free time?"

"Well," Helena said scanning Makoa's forearms and deciding how much she wanted to push this. Okay that was a lie, she always enjoyed pushing things. She put down her fork. "I like reading. And of course, sex is always a good time."

Makoa stilled and put his drink back down without taking a sip.

Oh he was cool under pressure. Helena liked that a lot. "What do you do for fun?" she asked quietly.

He leaned a bit closer. "Well, I have some friends who I play video games with. And I read. And I like sex too. The thing is good sex makes me sleepy."

Helena nodded. "Even when there's a chance for a repeat performance?"

Makoa swallowed. Oh she enjoyed watching him. Enjoyed that he considered everything she said carefully and didn't just jump in with a quip. "I wonder if they would let us take coffee to go?" He waved at the bartender. And they both paid their bills, and each got a coffee in a to go cup, and then they went upstairs to Helena's room.

The door swung shut behind them. Makoa pulled her close, kissing her. The buzzing attraction switched into high gear because now those arms tugged her close, and she could feel his chest against hers, and she wanted to feel more of him.

"Wow," Makoa said pulling away.

Helena smiled because wow. "Condoms," she said aloud so that he understood when she slipped around him. She had only partially unpacked, but the bag of toiletries sat on the bathroom counter. She grabbed several condoms, and then walked back out, kicking her shoes under the dresser.

"Unzip me?" she asked turning so he could see the zipper. She could reach the back of the dress herself, but this was part of the fun, part of the learning. Would he go slow or fast? Perfunctory or sensual?

Makoa leaned in and moved her hair out of the way. He pressed a kiss to her shoulder and then the back of her neck. Oh this man was going to kill her. Cause of death, extreme attraction. But what a way to go.

His hand moved to the zipper, and he moved slowly, undoing the zipper as carefully as if this was a game of Operation, and he had the tweezers.

She wished the zipper went further. This was a packing up the convention and then going to the airport dress, so the zipper stopped just past her waist.

He pressed a kiss to her back. And she shifted so that she could take her arms out of the dress, pushing it down and out of the way.

He moved his hands to the clasp on the back of her bra. "May I? he asked.

"Please," she said.

He undid the clasp and helped her slide the straps off. She tossed the dress and bra onto one of the two queen beds.

He pulled her in for another kiss, and she wiggled a little, enjoying the sensation of his kiss combined with the texture of his shirt against her naked breasts. She slid her hands down to his waist, tugging his shirt out of his pants, and sliding her hands under and up to feel the skin of his back.

When he shifted back, she asked, "May I?"

He nodded and she lifted the shirt up, standing on tiptoes, to get it over his head. She tossed that too. She looked at his pants, and his socks and shoes that were still on, and decided maybe she was done waiting.

"First one naked on the bed gets to come first?" she asked.

Makoa paused, thinking.

Helena skimmed off her underpants and leapt onto the bed. "I win!" she said.

MAKOA LAUGHED. HE TOOK his time getting the rest of his clothes off. If he'd lost, he'd lost, though the prize of making Helena come first was hardly a loss. Once his clothes were all off, he doubled checked the alarms on his phone and made sure the lids on their coffee were secure, resting on the desk.

He checked his hair in the mirror which also gave him a chance to see if Helena found this amusing or was about to kick him. He used to do this all the time as a kid. When his older sisters told him they had beaten him, he'd just mosey. Why hurry if he'd already lost.

Helena looked amused by his moseying. But he turned and faced her because while he wasn't above teasing, he also really did want his prize. Her prize. the prize of making her come.

He climbed onto the bed and moved up and kissed her. Their tongues met, and the heat built, so hot with the promise of more. He moved his hands over her shoulders, her arms, her breasts, feeling the texture of her skin, watching where she moaned or stilled as he touched. He kissed the parts she leaned into when he touched. His hands moved more, across her stomach, her hips, over her thighs.

He shifted to stroke her calves, her ankles. He slid his hands back up, teasing the backs of her knees, the insides of her thighs which she widened. "May I?" he asked, hands hovering over her center.

"Please," she said.

He settled between her legs, and pressed fingers on her labia, spreading her wider. He leaned down, adjusting his legs so he didn't fall off the edge of the mattress. He licked her center, tasting her swirling his tongue around her clit. He slid a finger, and then two inside her, as he continued to lick her clit. She brought a hand down, to rub herself and he watched as he continued to slide his fingers in and out.

Her groans changed pitch, and her thighs tightened and he picked up the pace, siding faster, adding a thumb to the pressure against her clit.

She came with a final moan, and he held himself still until he slid his fingers carefully away. Yeah, he definitely won with that prize.

After a moment, she reached for a condom. "Your turn," she said.

"Our turn," he corrected.

"That too," she said. She directed him to sit against the headboard.

"My thighs are kinda wide," he warned her.

"I work out," she said. She rolled the condom down his cock. She leaned in to kiss him. "How close are you?"

"Pretty close," he admitted.

"Excellent," she said. She shifted and then slid down onto him. He reached his hands under her butt to help her lever up and down. She grabbed his shoulders and tugged closer shifting the angle so that they both moaned.

Helena paused and then reached between them, stroking her hands over his chest, tugging his nipples, skimming over his arms, his sides.

"Helena," he said, afraid to use more words, but wanting to hurry.

"Sorry, just wanted to admire the scenery a bit."

He huffed a laugh.

She moved again, faster. He reached hand between them, working to rub her clit, feeling her tighten further around him. She moved faster, and he helped her, feeling the orgasm climb up his spine. He came in an explosive grunt, but managed to keep his hand moving over her clit until she followed.

"OKAY, MIGHT BE TIME for coffee, or maybe water," Helena said an orgasm or two later. She got up and grabbed her phone from her dress pocket. "Ah, the restaurant closed. So, tap water, or room temperature coffee it is."

"There should be a vending machine," Makoa said.

"Yeah, but it's an old one that takes actual cash. It did not like my cash."

"Oh wow," Makoa said. "That's surprising. I travel a lot for work, and I can't remember the last time I saw that. I always carry quarters though. I just keep them in my checked bag because it freaks out TSA. I can run get some."

"You can." Helena sipped the room temperature coffee. "But seriously, one night of tap water won't kill me."

Makoa tipped his head like he was running through a pro con list in real time. It was pretty cute. Or hot. In another ten minutes she'd find him hot again. They definitely had time for another round or two before they needed to clean up and get ready for the airport shuttle.

"Yeah," Makoa said getting up and grabbing his clothes from the other bed. "Let me do it. I can just bring my bags up here, if that's okay. And then we can just hop on the airport shuttle together. If you don't mind me brushing my teeth and all that in here."

Why she would mind that? "Sure," Helena said. "I'll be waiting here."

He slid on his clothes but carried his socks and shoes and slipped out, holding the door so it closed softly behind him. Helena grabbed her dress off the floor and packed it. She grabbed another outfit and placed on the hanger, so it would hopefully magically unwrinkle in the next three hours. She checked that there were still unused condoms out, and then poured herself a glass of tap water because hydration was important.

She startled awake and checked the time. Her phone alarm dinged. She looked around, but Makoa wasn't back. She was a light sleeper. She definitely would have heard him knocking. Which meant - well it meant he hadn't come back. It was weird but some people hated to be like that was fun, let's never speak again. But he could have just said he'd be back. No need to create a whole narrative about bringing his stuff if he was just going to be all, that was fun, bye.

She was more annoyed he lied about coming back if he wasn't going to, than that he didn't return.

Well, Helena wasn't in Colorado all that often anyway, so no big loss. She got some orgasms, had some fun. And now she was going to get ready to get to Vegas and soak up some time with her tutu.

Chapter 3

Makoa was having the worst day and it was barely breakfast time. "I need my bag," he said as politely as he could manage to the airline employee. His bag was well within carry on limits, but they had insisted he check it before boarding, and so he had handed it over. The kid next to him had spilled apple juice on him, which the very embarrassed parent had apologized profusely for. It wasn't anyone's fault, not even the kid, who had burst into tears at realizing he had done something that the adults were tense about.

But now the apple juice had dried into a sticky mess. He wanted to change before he showed up at the hotel or this would be all his family talked about for the weekend and possibly forever.

He also felt terrible about Helena, but he could barely even think about that right now. It turned out if you snuck quietly out of someone's hotel room in the middle of the night, you should definitely write their hotel room number down. Hotel clerks do not think kindly of dudes who want the names of someone's hotel room at three am. Which is good safety protocol that he appreciated on behalf of everyone. It was just very inconvenient when you hadn't exchanged phone information with the person.

But right now, he needed a clean shirt, and his clean shirts were in his bag. Which was not on the conveyor belt. And he was starting to get a sneaking suspicion it was not in Vegas at all.

"Did the bag get on the plane with me?" he asked keeping his voice quiet and as friendly as he could manage. He knew it wasn't this dude's fault. It was almost never the fault of the human in front of you. This was why he liked hockey. It was always clear who you could smash and who you could not.

"Um yeah," the airline employee said staring at the computer screen, "I have someone in Denver checking on that. It was tagged that it did. But, the runway team assures me there is nothing left on the plane."

What felt like an eternity later, Makoa had an apology, and still no bag. They were going to call him when it turned up. They assured him the bag wasn't lost, merely misplaced. There was nothing irreplaceable in the bag. But it was just another thing that had gone just a little wrong. He was going to find a cab driver who would take him somewhere that was not a hotel to buy some clothes.

He texted his mom that he was in Vegas just needed to make a stop before he met them at the hotel. One very excellent cab trip later, Makoa arrived at the hotel with clothes, underwear, and a small duffel in case his bag never showed up.

His mom sat in the breakfast buffet at a large table. Most of the other tables were cleared away, or had a few jetlagged or hungover folks lingering. It was near the end of the breakfast time.

He put his bag down and hugged his mom in her chair. "Hi, Ma. I made it."

"It's good of you to come. I know you have a lot to do in Colorado."

His mom always said Colorado like it was some sketchy place he had made the rash decision to move to. "I'm always glad to see you. And the rest of the family. The kids get too antsy?"

"They wanted to get in the pool the second it opened. Kids. Anyway, I need you to take me to a thing. It starts soon, but you have time to eat. Did you get your key? Are your bags in the room?"

"They didn't find my bag, so I stopped and got some stuff." He patted the bag.

"Do you have a shirt with buttons?"

Makoa wore a black t-shirt. He had bought three neutral-colored t-shirts. None of the button-down shirts he'd seen were wide enough for his chest and he didn't want to spend a lot of time looking. He figured the hotel wasn't that fancy. "My polo shirt has an apple juice stain on it, so I need to wash it."

"You spilled your juice?"

"It wasn't my juice."

"Well, I suppose the dark shirt looks okay. Grab some food but eat carefully. Can't have you running around on an empty stomach."

Makoa was not planning to do much running around today. The pool sounded like a great idea. But he was all for eating some food. At some point today he was going to need a nap. But food first.

A little while later, the hotel folks began packing up the food, and stripping down tables.

"Okay, Makoa, we need to get going." Makoa nodded and grabbed his bag, following his mom. He hoped they were headed to the room first. But if not, the bag wasn't that heavy. He was just more afraid of putting down somewhere and losing sight of it. Didn't want to lose a second bag in the same day.

As they wandered through hallways and made turns, Makoa wondered if he should have turned on the GPS or something. He was never going to remember how to get back to the dining hall or anywhere else. Maybe he should have grabbed some bread and left a trail of breadcrumbs.

"OH, YOU LOOK GREAT," Tutu said as Helena exited the bathroom. "Did you get enough to eat?"

Tutu had agreed Helena could treat them to in room breakfast, because after the airplane Helena needed a little break from humanity in large quantities. But now they were getting ready to go peek at the expo. "I did. Did you? We can go steal some last pastries from the buffet?"

"It's not stealing when we're staying in the hotel. But I'm okay. Let's head down now. I heard there might be gift bags for the first people to check in."

"Let me just grab my bathing suit."

"I know we're islanders, but you can't wear your suit to the expo."

"Haha. I know, Tutu. I just figured I'd get some pool time in before it starts. It's not supposed to start until noon." Helena gestured at the time on the hotel alarm clock.

"We can come back. I don't wanna miss."

Helena decided not to fight it. Even though with this large hotel it was going to take like twenty minutes to get back to the room, which was forty minutes of pool time. But who was she to stand in the way of free gift bags.

"Okay, let's go."

They ran into two families waiting for the elevator. The kids who looked to be maybe kindergarten-ish, all wore swim gear, with goggles and towels and even a snorkel.

Tutu chatted with the family while they waited, learning that they were here for the expo too, but were headed for the pool. Helena glanced meaningfully at Tutu, trying to convey - see, they are going to the pool first - but Tutu looked away.

Tutu and Helena got off on the conference room level. Helena scanned the signs, but Tutu kept walking. "Tutu, I think registration is over this way."

"I talked to Anu, she said to go this way."

"Okay," Helena said. She wished she just gone to the pool with the families. Unless the gift bag had a bathing suit. Which seemed doubtful. But she was getting time with Tutu, even if wandering around the conference level was not quite what she had planned.

"Are you ladies here for the show?" A guy in dark clothes with a walkie-talkie and tablet asked.

Show? Helena knew plenty of hotels in Vegas had theaters, but the Lovestar Hotel was off strip. It had pools and conference rooms. And an event space they claimed was perfect for weddings. But no shows.

"Yes," Tutu said, "This is Helena Smith."

Helena looked at Tutu. "Tutu, what-"

"Ah, excellent," walkie-talkie guy said. "Just in time. Let me take you over to where we're gathering the contestants. And then ma'am, we have a viewing area where we're allowing a small amount of family to view the taping. We have to keep you out of mic range though. I'm sure you understand."

Helena was quite sure she did not understand. Or worse, that she did.

Chapter 4

Makoa stood there as the production assistant miced him up. He felt surreal. It could be lack of sleep. Or it could be that ever since he wandered a hotel hallway in the middle of the night trying to figure out which door to knock on, he had known the universe had plans for him today.

He had not imagined: oh, my mom signed me up for a reality show, but why not. It wasn't even close to the weirdest or most annoying thing that had happened today.

"There's never been a reality show with all Hawaiian contestants, Muli Hope, don't you want to be part of history?" his mom had said.

And while it was tempting to point out he was trying to be part of history by being a Hawaiian pro hockey player, how could he say no? His mom had said it was just a test episode, a proof of concept for them to pitch to the TV stations. His sports agent would probably kill him. Makoa knew most things pitched to TV went nowhere, so he figured he'd just maybe not tell his sports agent and deal with the fallout if it somehow actually did get on TV. Which it wouldn't. He'd do a silly challenge. And then he could go nap at the pool. Let the sun bake away his residual feelings about missing out on anything more with Helena. Oh and enjoy being with his family. Even if his mom was currently pimping him out to TV shows.

The assistant moved him over to a door. "Wait here. We'll lead everyone in about five minutes."

It was more like fifteen, not that Makoa was counting. He hadn't done many interviews as a minor league player. But he had been through media training and they had told them there was a lot of hurry up and wait. He had hoped his mom was leading him somewhere with snacks. Sure, he had just eaten breakfast, but it took a lot of protein to keep him fully fueled. And sleep. If he couldn't get a nap, maybe the show would be about food. He was a passable cook, and he could sneak some of the food while he was cooking.

The assistant came back and led him to the backside of a tall structure that Makoa guessed was the backside of the set. "Okay, you're next - walk around, wave or something, go stand behind the next contestant."

Makoa nodded and walked out into the brightly lit ballroom. There were counters and stovetops, so he might luck out with this food idea. An announcer said, "And here we have Makoa Wilson, currently living in Colorado, but raised in Nevada, where his parents moved from Maui."

Makoa waved and moved to stand next to a tall dude, who was lined up next to some other dudes. Peeking around he saw a line of women contestants on the other end of the room. He wondered if they were setting them up for gender pairs or a gender face off. If they were only accounting for two genders, while claiming to be a Hawaiian show about real Hawaiians, Makoa didn't think much of the show. But maybe they had more surprises in store.

"And now our host, the one, the only, the legend, Lili Hae!"

One of the production assistants mimed clapped at them and they all clapped. Makoa had heard of Lili Hae. Lili was a kumu hula, an activist, a comedian, and a generally amazing human. Well, that's what Makoa got for thinking the show was gonna be basic.

"Aloha! Aloha to all of you at home, those of you who've come to witness this historic moment, and those of you brave enough to sign up to compete in our games today. You've already met our lovely contestants. I'm going to let you on a little secret, a little behind the scenes stuff. Right now, we are in Las Vegas, in our lovely space here at the Lovestar Hotel, isn't that a great name, the Lovestar Hotel? Anyway, right now it is July. And July makes you think many things, beaches, cocktails, vacations, sun, but one thing that it might not make you think is Christmas!"

At the word, the main lights in the room dimmed. and the large potted palm trees along the back of the set lit up with multicolored twinkle lights.

The room lights brightened back up and Lili said, "But one thing Hawaiians know, is that heat, sun, and the beach, are exactly how we celebrate Christmas. So, there's a song about twelve days of Christmas. You might have heard it. But there's a Hawaiian version of it too. That's right no drummer boys in our version, which is a shame, because I do love a little drummer boy." Lili winked.

Makoa wasn't sure if he was allowed to laugh, but well, Lili was great fun.

"So, our lovely contestants are going to run through some challenges inspired by the Hawaiian version of the song. First up, we have some papaya trees!"

Two production assistants wheeled potted papaya trees out and placed them on either side of Lili. Paper birds dangled from each tree.

"As you can see, our trees came with mynah birds already in them. I asked for real mynah birds, but apparently TV viewers don't like watching birds poop on the contestants or something. So paper will have to do."

One of the contestants from the other side walked up to Lili.

"Ah, the lovely Chanel has come over to help demonstrate. Chanel if you could please select a mynah bird from the tree."

Chanel chose one.

"Please hold that up for the camera."

Chanel did. A camera person zoomed in on the paper bird.

"Okay, the mynah bird has a number. The mynahs on this tree, all have numbers that match the mynahs on this tree. So, if we could all come forward and make our selection."

They moved towards the trees. Makoa spotted his mom watching over head. She waved at him when she saw him looking. He smiled back. The guy behind him nudged him, and Makoa moved forward. Once he had his mynah bird, he looked for the number. Four. Some people thought it was unlucky, but he had always liked it and it was in fact his jersey number. Maybe things were turning around for him.

Lili had everyone hold up their number so everyone could pair up. He could see a person holding four fingers up, but the tall guy was in the way. He scooted around and saw - it was Helena.

HELENA LOOKED AT MAKOA in disbelief. "You," she said. She remembered she was miced and on camera. She was willing to be on a reality show. But she was not going to create drama for the show. No sir. She was not mining her emotions for free.

She smiled brightly. And nodded as everyone settled into their pairs facing Lili. Makoa's hand reached for hers and she shifted away reaching her hand up to smooth her hair and then placing her arms clasped behind her back.

"So," Lili said. "We have mynah birds, no longer in papaya trees, but you can never trust a mynah bird to stay put. Ask me how I know. Do any of our contestants remember the next present?"

"Coconuts," Helena said along with several other contestants who clearly had an island themed holiday playlist going in their households too. Her parents always used to say they left the islands, but the islands didn't leave them.

"That's right my little coconuts, coconuts are next. So, we have several stations set up. And you each have a coconut for you and your partner to crack open. It has been lovely having so many of you here with us. But I am sorry to inform you that this is a timed challenge. We will only be allowed to take the top six pairs into our next challenge.

So, once we have everyone in place, you will want to get to cracking quickly."

Helena wanted to ask if the pairs were going to be stuck with each other for the rest of the challenge. She wasn't above throwing the challenge and going back to having more pool time with her tutu. She looked up at the balcony full of watchers above and her tutu was giving her a thumbs up. Well, shoot, okay maybe she was too stubborn to throw the very first challenge.

They were each directed to a rolling cart set up with a coconut.

"Now," Lili said. "We've made it easy for you all. These coconuts have already been taken from the tree and de-husked. We've practically done all the work for you. When you finish yell 'pau pono' and we'll mark the time and then come check your work. The coconut needs to be cracked open, and the meat accessible."

A tall contestant raised his hand.

"Do you have a question?" Lili asked.

"Does it matter if we save the milk or just getting it cracked open counts?"

"Oh that's such a good question. We are prioritizing speed, but because I can, let me just say I'll give special bonus to the first pair to have all the milk saved too. Oh, and I don't know if you were frisked properly before you entered our arena here. But the only tools you can use are on the bottom of your cart. We'll be watching. Okay, everybody ready? The time starts now!"

Helena looked under the cart. There was a screwdriver, a mallet, and a plastic bowl.

She placed them all on the top of the cart next to the coconut. "So, how much experience do you have with coconuts, because I usually buy them already canned."

"My grandparents had a coconut tree and I once was dared by my cousins to shimmy up and grab a coconut. But on the tree, they have an outer husk. Also, my mom was the one who cracked it open, I just retrieved it."

"Pau pono!" someone yelled.

"Okay," Helena said, "well, as much as I like special bonuses, it looks like speed is going to be our priority here. So, is the screwdriver for leverage and then we pound?"

Helena looked around trying to tell what everyone else was doing. But most of them were standing in such a way that she couldn't see the coconut, just their hunched backs. Rude.

"Well, the coconut should have these eyes things." Makoa held the coconut, running his fingers over the shell. "And so, you poke at the eyes to get the milk out." He grabbed the screwdriver and poked it in.

"Pau pono!" another team yelled.

"Yes," Makoa said, and held the coconut over the bowl as liquid trickled out.

"Okay," Helena said. "I guess we're aiming for the bonus." She was a little annoyed he just steamrolled right over what she said. But this was Makoa, not exactly a trustworthy dude at this point. So, her priority was getting through this challenge.

She smiled at a camera person hovering nearby.

"Pau pono" another team yelled.

Helena had lost count, but there were definitely only a few spots left. "Okay, we may need to start cracking. We're running low on time."

"Patience," Makoa said tipping the coconut. Liquid continued to trickle out.

Helena really hated to be told to be patient, especially on a timed challenge. Patience was not on the menu. But what was she going to do. Wrestle the coconut away?

"Pau pono!" another team yelled.

"We need to crack unless you want to go home in the first challenge," she said.

"Pau pono!" someone yelled. Helena was getting tired of hearing that.

Makoa shook the coconut one more time, then set it on the cart, screwdriver still in place. "I'll hold it, you hammer."

It took all Helena had not to say, "that's what he said" to that statement. Makoa did not deserve good dirty jokes at this point. She tapped the screwdriver with the mallet.

"Close," he said.

She tapped with a little more force. The coconut cracked open and she raised her hand yelling, "Pau pono!" right as another team did.

A production assistant raced over and wrote something down on their tablet. "Oh, you got the water too. Nice job."

"Okay folks," another production assistant yelled. "Talk amongst yourselves for a moment. We're going to check the time stamps and review everyone's work. Don't move from your station yet. Thank you!"

"Helena, I tried to come back -" Makoa said.

Helena held up her hand in a stop motion. "Don't. Not now. Not here." Possibly not ever, but that was a discussion they could have, or not have really, later. She was too keyed up with adrenaline from this silly challenge to trust herself. Also, there were mics and cameras. Her emotions were not for TV, and not for Makoa. He had done nothing to earn them.

Chapter 5

Makoa wanted to explain everything to Helena now. But sure, maybe in a large ballroom in a hotel while they filmed a reality show was not the best time. But the universe had given Helena to him as a teammate for a reason. He just had to figure out when the optimal time was. Before she ran away.

"Okay," Lili said." Lili sat in an elaborate red chair on top of a raised staircase, the papaya trees on either side. "It looks like we have a tie, with the final two teams. So, we are going to have a coconut off. We have Helena and Makoa and Clay and Opal. We are going to bring you four up front here, and to make things a little more interesting, we are taking away the tools.

The production assistant waved them forward to a large area with several tarps spread out on the floor.

"We will reset the clock and the first to crack their coconut gets to join the other teams in the next challenge."

Helena's hand shot up.

"Question?"

"So, does no tools include shoes?"

"Oh, excellent question. Shoes can be used. But no other tools or clothing you may have with you today. Body parts are of course allowed. But remember folks, we're trying to keep it family friendly in here, so please stick to visible body parts. Okay any other questions? Great. Time starts now!"

"You're taller," Helena said, "so you hold it up high and drop it. Or smash it."

"You're not going to use your shoes?"

"Not if you can drop it fast."

Makoa glanced over and saw the other team was trying to use a shoe to crack it open. Makoa held the coconut up high and tried to drop it with enough force to crack it open. It bounced and rolled on the tarp.

He reached down but Helena grabbed his arm and stomped on the coconut. "Pau pono!" she yelled.

The production assistant nodded and signaled to Lili. "And we have a winner. Clay and Opal, if you can join the other teams over here. And Makoa and Helena if you can join these teams on this side of me."

They moved over.

Lili said, "Well, my coconuts, thank you for joining us on this first episode of 'The Next Great Hawaiian'. I am sorry to say that today is your last day of Christmas. Aloha and Mele Kalikimaka to you." The losing teams followed a production assistant out.

Makoa leaned over, "Did you ask about the shoe to throw off the other team?"

Helena smiled. "We used my shoe."

True. But he was pretty sure that smile was the smile of a devious plan seen to fruition. As a muli hope he knew that smile well. People thought as an athlete, Makoa would be competitive about everything. Being the muli hope with two older sisters he had learned to lose often. So, he hadn't been sure he was going to try that hard in this competition. But if it got Helena to smile at him, then he definitely wanted to keep playing.

THEY'D BEEN SENT TO another ballroom set up with curtained off areas to change. Tutu had retrieved her bag, so Helena had all her clothes. She was getting into this show. A nap, or lunch soon would be nice, but this was fun too. It wasn't exactly what she had imagined for the Hawaiian Expo, but the expo itself was mostly booths and a few workshops. The fun was in the chance to meet and be near so many other Hawaiians. And she was getting to do that with the show, even if so far she had only met Makoa.

She was still annoyed with him. It didn't matter what stopped-to-rescue-a-kitten excuse he had. When you bail or ghost someone, that was it. Helena was great at meeting and finding new people to hang out with. She didn't need to waste time with folks who couldn't be trusted to be straightforward.

Sure, he was very good in bed, and she had made exceptions for that before. And the t-shirt he wore now, proved her theory that the polo shirt had not been doing him any favors.

But he had ignored her input during the first part of the challenge. Though he had listened during the coconut off, even picked up her strategy.

But no. There were ten other contestants that were not her or Makoa. She had plenty of new friends to make.

Back in the challenge ballroom, as Helena was coming to think of it, there was now a station with six induction burners. And a line of carts each with a cloche on it along with kitchen utensils and bowls underneath.

A cooking challenge. Helena could cook, she just didn't get excited about combining ingredients or adding spices. She was a great eater if someone else wanted to do all the cooking. She looked up and Tutu waved again making a thumbs up sign. Helena was going to do her best. To make herself proud, to make Tutu proud, and maybe to make Makoa regret how much he missed out on.

The production assistants gathered the contestants in front of the stair podium. Lili came in, also in a new outfit, and waved climbing onto the podium. "Okay, my little coconuts, we have made it through the first two days of Christmas. Hopefully you all are starting to feel the Christmas aloha. The Kalikimaka aloha." Lili winked. "Now, for our next challenge, we are going to combine a few of the days. But first, if you each could select a mynah bird."

There was only one papaya tree this time. The each went forward and selected a mynah bird.

"We'll be doing teams again. The good news is this time only one team will be eliminated. Each of the carts has a number on it. It will help you find your station, and your teammate for this challenge."

Helena found her cart. Her partner was a very tall woman. "Hi, I'm Eliza," she said.

"Helena."

"Contestants," Lili said, "you may look under the cloche."

Eliza grabbed the silver top, and underneath it sat a bowl of - Helena wasn't quite sure - it was food. She saw ham, bacon, something else that was lighter in color than the bacon. And shrimp.

Eliza clapped her hand over her mouth.

"Contestants, that's right, we have dried squid and some pig products to represent our big fat pigs, poor things. I had suggested we grease some pigs and let you all try to catch them, but apparently the Lovestar Hotel frowns on that. So instead, we eat. Or I will eat, once you all prepare something for me. You are going to have 1 hour, and access to the pantry over there, and the burners. Use your time wisely and make us all proud."

Lili waved and then came down from her podium.

The large clock started counting the seconds as they ticked by.

"Any ideas?"

"I am allergic to shellfish," Eliza said.

"Okay, are you going to be able to help cook or no you need to leave now?"

"I don't think I can touch anything, but I can help brainstorm, I guess."

"Okay. I'm going to run over to the pantry and see what our options are." Helena went over. She passed one contestant carrying twelve cans of coconut milk, which seemed like hoarding. Helena might have been the tiniest bit shady with her shoe question, but she hadn't hoarded tools. She had mostly wanted to make sure she wasn't disqualified for stepping on the coconut. The fact that the other team misunderstood her intent was really a bonus.

She grabbed a few eggs, holding them carefully so others could use the carton. She found some cheese, a sweet potato, and some garlic. She looked at the taro, but she seemed to recall that taro needed a longer cook time and they were on a time crunch so she left it.

Back at the cart, she showed Eliza her choices. "I'm thinking omelet of sorts. It's not fancy, but we can get it done in time."

"Sure. I can slice the potato and garlic for you."

"Thanks." Helena cracked the eggs and stirred them up, tossing in some salt, pepper, and other spices from the bottom of the cart.

Eliza handed her the chopped potato, and Helena went over to the cooking station. She grabbed a large skillet and tossed the bacon in first. When that finished, she put the bacon aside to cool, and put the sweet potato in the skillet. Once that was starting to sear, she added the shrimp and garlic, and then the dried squid. She saved some dried squid for later. And then she added the egg mixture. She turned the heat down. They still had some time left, and she didn't want to be done too soon and have the omelet sit there. But she didn't want to overcook it either.

"An omelet, so predictable," a contestant near her said.

"What are you making?" she asked politely.

"A frittata," the contestant said.

Helena was pretty sure that unless you baked it, it was an omelet. But whatever.

"I'm hoping for cake," another contestant said.

"I've got ratatouille," another said.

"I'm not telling," one contestant said.

Helena looked around. Makoa stood at his station with his partner kneading something. She checked the clock. She hoped they weren't planning to cook that. There were only about ten minutes left.

Helena checked her omelet. It was starting to get crisp around the edges. She turned the heat down as low as she could, shaking the pan to make sure it stayed loose and didn't stick.

With five minutes left, she lifted the skillet off the burner, grabbed the bacon, to go back to her station.

Makoa raced to the burner and grabbed a pan, turning the flame up high.

"Careful," another contestant said.

Helena squelched her curiosity and went back to her station where Eliza had two plates set out. She divided the omelet and put a little dried squid and bacon topping on each.

"Can I take it?" a production assistant asked. Helena and Eliza nodded and he took it over to where they were taking glamour shots of the food.

"I wish he'd bring it back, I never had lunch," Helena said.

Eliza clapped her hand over her mouth again.

"Sorry. Maybe they'll let us make lunch when the challenge is done. Shellfish free."

"Medic!" someone yelled.

Helena looked over. A contestant clutched their hand with a napkin wrapped around it.

She glanced over to Makoa who looked around and looked at her. She turned and looked back at Eliza. And tried not to feel anything about Makoa looking over, maybe to make sure she was okay. Hopefully dude with the napkin on his hand would be okay. She felt a little bad for being glad it wasn't Makoa.

After much conferring the contestant's hand was bandaged and gloved. They stood behind their station with their challenge partner.

Lili came back out. And walked over to the glamour shot area, where she started eating.

Oh, Helena guessed that made sense, for her to eat everything hot while it was still hopefully warm. A production assistant followed her with a tablet, making notes.

Then Lili came and started making her way to each station, followed by a camera. She chatted. The mics seemed to be set not to project, so it was hard to hear what she said. Helena started to feel her stomach churn with nervousness. It was just a silly TV show. She made it through the first challenge. If she went home now for making a basic omelet, it would be fine. She'd get to sip cocktails by the pool with her tutu.

She glanced over to Eliza who held her hand over her mouth again.

Lili made it to them and said, "Oh an omelet."

Helena couldn't tell if that was oh another omelet or oh, how original, or oh, I was hoping someone would make an omelet. But she smiled.

"And you put the dried squid on top. Is there some in the omelet too?"

"There is," Helena said.

"Well, you definitely used everything. Now Eliza, a little mynah birdie told me you didn't help as much with the cooking. Was that division of labor your decision or Helena's?"

"I'm allergic to shellfish, so Helena kindly agreed to take on a lot of the cooking so that I didn't run into issues."

"Oh goodness. Well, I'm glad you didn't have any allergic reactions. And Helena were you okay doing most of the cooking."

"Eliza helped with the prep, and we didn't need two of us to stand over the burner. Everything worked great."

"Happy, happy. That's what we like to hear. Oh that's a lie. I love mess." Lili waved and moved to the next station.

Eliza let out a huge breath. "Do you mind - could you move that plate away?"

"Sure," Helena said. She walked over and stuck it next to the other glamour shot plates. She scanned the plates, the frittata, the ratatouille, the cake, and what looked like a fry bread topped with shrimp and bacon. Wow, that plate looked great. She counted again. There were only five plates. But six teams.

A production assistant shooed her back to her station with Eliza. Eliza appeared to be doing slow breathing. She thought about telling Eliza there were only five plates, but she remembered she was still miced up, so she stayed quiet.

"Well, my coconuts," Lili said back in her stair podium. "Thank you so much for making me lunch. Ha! My favorite was the bacon fry bread with the shrimp and squid ceviche. So great job there, Makoa and David. Unfortunately, Ed and Randy were not able to finish their dish due to injury, so we are going to have to say goodbye to them. Ed and Randy, this is your last day of Christmas. Aloha and Mele Kalikimaka."

The camera person moved close to them and followed them as they exited the ballroom.

Lili passed her mic to a production assistant. "For the rest of you we are going to break for lunch. We have invited the family and friends that have been watching us to join. Please don't leave the conference area. We don't want to hunt you down."

Lili waved a pageant wave, and walked away. Helena hoped Tutu was coming down to join everyone for lunch. Partly because that was the real reason she was here in Vegas and not home recovering from the work conference. But also, she wasn't ready to face Makoa somewhere they could talk. Not yet.

Chapter 6

"You're doing great, Muli Hope," Makoa's mom said. They sat at one of the tables set up in the ballroom where contestants had been changing and waiting. The hotel had set up a selection of food.

"Thanks, Mom," Makoa said. I though you said they were doing like one episode."

"Yeah, they apparently decided to do the whole series while they had all these willing contestants here. But you're having fun, right?"

"It is fun. But I'm not getting to see you all. Are the sisters and all them still at the pool?"

"I think they said something about going to visit the sharks. But don't worry. We'll see them at dinner."

Makoa had a sneaking suspicion his family had all known he'd be doing this thing. He had talked about wanting to go see the shark display at one of the casinos but his sisters had kept being like we'll see how the kids feel. Which fine. His niblings would have definitely been bored out of their minds watching this show.

"How did you even find out about the show?" he asked.

"Oh, your Auntie Nene mentioned it. She saw it on the computer."

Makoa's mom was perfectly savvy with the internet, had accounts on multiple social media platforms, and often told him what was trending. When she said things like the computer, it meant she was pretending she couldn't remember where. Which okay. He was here, he was doing it. He was even enjoying himself, although it would help if he could talk to Helena and not just watch her from across the room.

He and his partner had come up with the ceviche part easily. But David pointed out that if they didn't make something that needed to be cooked, they'd be dinged. Makoa had a fry bread recipe memorized, but it had taken a little longer to get the dough the right consistency in the dry hotel ballroom. He had realized everyone else was chatting over the burners, and he was kneading dough. This next challenge he'd figure out a way to talk. Even if Helena would only let him talk about the weather.

He'd have tried sitting next to her for lunch, but she and her grandmother, he was guessing, had taken their food to a corner, where there was no other seating. Message received.

"Do you know her?" Mom asked.

"The woman I was partnered with in the first challenge?' Makoa asked. "Not well."

"You met her before today?" Mom asked.

Makoa paused. The mic packs had come off for lunch, but they were still surrounded by people in the show. No one had asked him if he knew any of the contestants, so there was no reason to think it was against the rules for them to know each other. But he had also watched enough reality shows to know that revealing data like that often led to the producers plotting shenanigans. And he needed no more shenanigans when it came to Helena. And he hadn't known Helena for twenty-four hours even yet, so it wasn't really a lie to say he just met her today. "Just met her today."

"Ah, but you like her. I'll ask around."

"Mom, I don't need you to do that." He knew he had no chance of changing what his mother was going to do, he just wanted it on record. He wanted the info he gathered on Helena to come from her. And maybe this competition was the best way for him to get that.

Because while he had only known her for a day, he wanted to get to know her better. The show was fun, but it also gave him an excuse to keep being near Helena. And that was worth missing out on seeing the sharks.

"ARE YOU HAVING FUN?" Tutu asked. "Because it looks fun."

"I am," Helena said. She wouldn't mind a nap. But she felt just competitive enough that she'd grabbed a soda and would power through.

"Oh good. I wish I could have signed myself up for it. But they wanted to start with all young people."

"Silly them. I bet you'd have opened those coconuts much faster."

"Well, you and your man got it done."

Helena rolled her eyes at her Tutu but smiled so she didn't get bopped in the head for disrespect. Makoa was not her man any more than Eliza was her woman. She glanced back, hoping Eliza had found some non-shellfish food to enjoy. She kept her eyes moving so she didn't accidentally linger on Makoa who was eating with someone she assumed was his mom.

Eliza was sitting with some other contestants eating. Helena realized maybe not everyone had come to the expo with family. She'd ask whoever she got paired up with next, assuming they kept to pairs for the next challenge.

"Oh, no pressure," Tutu said as they took their plates to toss them, "but I have a small bet going on who gets the furthest into the competition."

"No pressure, but my saintly grandmother's hard earned retirement money is riding on this? Okay, Tutu. Gambling, I never." She made an exaggerated pearl clutching pose.

"We are in Vegas, Keiki. Also, I know you'll do well, and I can take you out to dinner with my winnings."

"Well, I look forward to dinner then," Helena said. She hugged Tutu, feeling the good squeeze and wishing she could bottle this feeling. You couldn't hug over video chat.

The production assistants gathered everybody back in the room. The papaya tree was back next to the stair podium. Helena was starting to have feelings about that papaya tree. She probably should have gotten Tutu to sing the song with her on the lunch break so she could have planned ahead for what might be coming next. Oh, well, too late now.

Lili arrived back out in a new outfit.

"Aloha, my coconuts. We have a bigger challenge ready for this next round. So we did squid, and pigs, but we skipped over lei."

A production assistant wheeled out a long table full of flowers, and also some supplies. Helena spotted string for sure.

"But I would expect that stringing lei would be fairly easy for you all, so we have a little more to this challenge."

Another production assistant wheeled out a table full of 'ukulele.

Helena had had a 'ukulele as a kid. Had loved playing around with it. But she hadn't touched one in a while. She wasn't even sure where her old one was. Somewhere at her parents' house maybe. Her fingers itched to play it.

"That's right, we're going to ask you to play 'ukulele. And what would a good 'ukulele song be without a little hula. Yes, we are just racing through these days of Christmas. But I never much liked waiting to unwrap things." Lili winked.

"So, a few notes about how we're going to judge this. You and your partner will need to make a least one lei. Open or closed, it's all up to you. You will need to play the 'ukulele and hula while wearing said lei. Who is playing, who is dancing, who is wearing lei, these things are all up to you. Also, if only one of you is dancing, we do not care what gender that person is. If you want to make more lei, or figure out how both of you can hula and play 'ukulele, that will all be factored in. Also, while yes, I am a kumu hula, I brought in some guest judges to help me out with the other parts."

Lili stepped down from the stair podium and was joined by two people. A grey-haired dude in an aloha shirt and chinos. And a woman who looked familiar to Helena, wearing a floral dress. "First we have Vernon Raymond, also known as the Big V, who will help consult on the musical element of your performance. And Adriana, also known at the Pua Princess, who will help consult on the lei you make. Okay, any questions?"

A tall dude raised his hand. "So the more leis, the more points."

Lili smiled. "Our judging is going to encompass all three pieces. But yes, making multiple lei is one thing we will consider. But if you only make lei and don't play or dance, you will not move forward. Any more questions?"

Helena shook her head.

They were instructed to grab a mynah bird again. Helena didn't know what to wish for as she grabbed one so just picked the closest one and then held up her hand with the number 3.

"Hi, I'm Blake, they/them pronouns," they held up their mynah bird with a three. They wore a button-down blue shirt and chinos.

"Helena, she/her is fine. I'm not picky about pronouns at least."

"Gotta be picky about some things, right?"

"Exactly," Helena said.

"Everybody found their partner?" a production assistant asked. "Okay then you will have two hours for prep. We're going to use the second ballroom. There are lei supplies in there too. Teams one, two, and three are going to practice in here. Teams four and five are going to come with me to the other room. Teams four and five grab a ʻukulele on your way out."

"There are eight ʻukuleles in the song," Blake said, "you think they'd at least let us have a ʻukulele a piece."

"True, so you know the song well?" Helena asked.

"I do," Blake said. "My brain is ridiculously stuffed full of song lyrics. It's like my own personal playlist."

"Oh good, because I can play ʻukulele, but it always takes me a while to remember the lyrics."

"Then you go pick a ʻukulele, I'll grab some lei supplies."

"Sounds good." Helena went to look at the table. And if she noticed that Makoa and his partner were in the other ballroom, well, she was just making sure she didn't accidentally bump into him. Nothing more.

Chapter 7

Makoa was a little bummed not have been paired with Helena again. But Eliza seemed nice. And she had worked with Helena, so maybe she knew something. Though admittedly, he had not learned that much about David, so maybe not.

"I got called out for not participating enough in the last challenge, although I was allergic, and so that was kind of a little ableist," Eliza said. "Well, anyway. I need to participate a lot this challenge. Do you know how to make lei? It can't be that hard, right, there's like string and flowers, do you tie the flowers on?"

"Do you drink coffee?" Makoa asked.

"I drank a shit ton of coffee because I just got in from Japan and I am jet-lagged to hell. Am I talking too much? That sometimes happens when I have had too much caffeine or am tired."

"You're fine," Makoa said. She was talking a lot, but he tended to process slow. Plus making her nervous seemed like it wouldn't help. "Oh, you asked if I had made lei. I have, though it was the school kid kind where we did it with yarn. But I can sew, so I figure I can make a lei."

They grabbed lei supplies and put it with their ʻukulele.

"Do we want to each make a lei while we talk plan?" Makoa took a seat at the table where they laid out their stuff.

"Yeah, that sounds good," Eliza said.

It took a bit to figure out the best strategy for making the lei, but Makoa's sewing skills did turn out to be useful. "Don't close yours," Eliza said.

"I can leave it open," Makoa said. "But for hula, most people wear the closed ones."

"Oh shoot, you're right. Well, you can do whichever."

"I can leave it open for now. It could be good to have different styles."

"Oh, I wonder if I can make a lei po'o. It's just smaller. I should be able to do that." She held a length of string up to her head."

"We should probably talk about hula. Do you play 'ukulele?"

"I mostly played violin. But I could try. Do you play?"

"I played guitar in school for a bit."

"Were you in a band?"

"No, I played sports too much to be in a band." It was also why he had stopped playing. Being on buses to hockey games, too many people were trying to sleep. They did not appreciate live musical accompaniment. So the guitar stayed in his room, which meant it didn't get used much. It was back at his mom's. He still had a lot of stuff stored there, until he got called up.

"Well, try playing it."

He grabbed the 'ukulele and strummed a bit, getting used to the sounds. He tried a chord. Okay, the chords were higher on the 'ukulele, but the shapes to make with his hand were coming back to him. He strummed a few in succession. Aw yeah.

"Are you playing a Christmas song? In July?"

"It's on theme," Makoa said.

"True. Actually, hmm, do you know 'The Twelve Days of Christmas (Hawaiian Style)', it's a suck up choice, but we are being judged."

Across the room, the other team began strumming and singing "The Twelve Days of Christmas (Hawaiian Style)".

"Ah, okay, I can dance better than that, but it does seem like maybe everyone will go for the suck up song. Wait, what about the one about the beach and the sandman. Crap, what's that one called." Eliza started humming.

"I think I can do 'Mele Kalikimaka,'" Makoa said.

"Hi," a production assistant said. "'Mele Kalikimaka', the song that is, not the phrase, is still under copyright. So, if you could try to stick to older songs that would be great so we don't have to edit around your music."

Makoa nodded.

"That song is older than I am. It's older than my parents. What songs are older than that?" Eliza said.

Makoa noticed the team playing "Twelve Days of Christmas (Hawaiian Style)" also stopped playing. "We're screwed."

"Well, we could always do a regular Christmas song. Those are all out of copyright by now, right?"

"I think so. Maybe 'Winter Wonderland'? That's at least got a story. There's a Hawaiian version of it too, but that may not be out of copyright."

"Probably not."

Makoa figured out the chords and Eliza came up with some moves. "I'm so used to doing group hula, this is weird."

"Well, let me see if I can stand and play, then maybe I can do some moves with you."

They managed to work out some choreography. Makoa couldn't do any hand motions and play 'ukulele, but with the two of them together, it didn't look terrible. They found a mirror so they could see what they looked like together.

"Okay, this is good," Eliza said. "I think we should make more lei."

"Sure," Makoa said. The giant clock ticking in the room showed about thirty minutes left.

They each grabbed some string. Eliza kept holding hers up to her head, trying to measure.

Makoa decided to stick to another for around his neck.

And he wondered how Helena was doing. If she was going to hula. And if he was going to get to watch her perform. He still wanted to explain what had happened this morning. But he suspected his interest in Helena was more than that. She didn't live near Colorado, but he traveled plenty during the season, he could figure out how to stop in DC. It wasn't just the sex. Okay it was the sex, and also, he wanted to know more about her. Including if she would hula, play 'ukulele or both.

HELENA HAD A FANTASTIC time working with Blake. And yet, nerves churned in her stomach when their time came to present to the judges. She resisted looking up. She knew her tutu would give her a thumbs up, but right now it just felt like more pressure.

Blake gave her a supportive nod and they moved into the room. They saw the prior two contestants walking away but it was hard to tell how they felt. Helena did her best to push all of that away and focus only on the judges.

"Blake and Helena. What have you got for us?" Lili said.

"We're going to do a little story hula." Blake said.

Helena began strumming chords on the 'ukulele. "In the beginning, there were stars," she said. "When the star goddess and the sky god mated, they eventually created a human. Haloa, the first human."

"Haloa was brother to the taro plant." Blake bent down and made planting motions with his hands. "And so, when we eat taro, we honor our relatives." He made motions like he was eating two finger poi." Blake bowed to the judges.

Helena did too.

"Mahalo," they both said.

And then they waited. Blake had said for TV they weren't going to show a whole long performance, so shorter was better. Helena agreed in theory, but now the nerves whirled in her stomach. They had talked about songs, until the PA told them the show didn't have a music budget for anything still under copyright. There were plenty of older chants, Hawaiian songs, but without their phones, neither Blake or Helena could remember enough.

"So, that was rather short," Lili said.

"We were aiming for not boring the judges," Helena said.

"I appreciate that," Lili said. "My other judges, any questions?"

"So," The Big V asked. "Short can be good. I noticed you sort of skipped over the whole Wakea was actually Ho'ohokukalani's dad bit. Was that intentional or could you not remember their names?"

"We could remember their names," Blake said.

He was being kind because Helena had definitely not remembered their names until Blake reminded her.

"But," Black said, 'we felt that in a short story getting into ancient genealogy was maybe too much."

"So, if I asked you Ho'ohokukalani's name?"

"Big V," Lili said. "They don't have to answer questions about what they did not present."

"It's Papahanamoku," Blake said.

"Ah, very good," Big V said.

"If I may ask," Adriana said. "How did you decide who would play and who would hula?"

"I have a 'ukulele at home," Helena said. "And Blake went to a halau as a kid. Sorry, Blake, you can tell them."

"Yeah, I went to a halau for a little while. I mostly did group hula. But I was willing to be our dancer today."

"You have the hula posture, very strong movements," Lili said. "Okay, I think that's all we needed. Mahalo."

They walked off and followed into the other ballroom where the production assistant led them to the cluster of contestants. "Don't go anywhere. We have two more performances to go, then we'll do judging."

"I couldn't tell anything," Blake said. "Could you tell?"

Helena shook her head. "Like I'm pretty sure they didn't hate it. But other than that?" She shrugged.

She looked at the other contestants. Everyone looked tired. Lunch seemed kind of far away. She didn't know anyone else's name yet, other than Chanel. Well, she knew Makoa and Eliza, but they were apparently one of the contestant teams who hadn't performed yet.

"I kind of want to make more lei while we're just sitting here," one of the contestants, who had long dark hair said.

"Yeah, just sitting without phones is so hard," said another.

"We could play konane. Anyone got anything we could use for the pieces?" Blake said. "Oh wait. We could use the flowers."

Blake went over to the table and came back with an armful of flowers and leaves. "Flowers versus leaves. Anyone remember how many pieces it's supposed to be?"

"It varies," Chanel said. "It just needs to be a square."

Blake laid out a square with alternating flowers and leaves. The girl who had been bored came and sat across from him. Once the board was laid out, she took one of the leaves away and stacked it.

One of the productions assistants move closer to see what all they were doing and then wandered back.

Blake chose a flower to hop over a leaf. Helena scooched closer to watch. This was definitely better than staring at the walls or the clock.

"You have no strategy," one of the other contestants said.

"Or is that my strategy?" bored girl said. She hopped her leaf over a flower and removed the flower.

They kept removing pieces.

"Aha," the bored woman crowed, leaping her leaf over another flower.

Scanning the board, Helena saw that Blake had no pieces in position to hop.

"Yeah, I think I'm out. Who wants to take my place?"

No strategy dude immediately scooched in.

"I think she can take him," Blake said.

Strategy dude was trying to go in rows. But the bored woman kept hoping at the edges which interfered with his careful planning. It was chaos, but she looked like organized chaos.

"I think you might be right," Helena said.

"I'm willing to put a flower on him," Chanel said.

"I guess, I'll put a leaf on her," Helena said. Blake handed them each a flower and a leaf.

"Are you guys still making lei?" Eliza asked. "Oh, we are playing a game and gambling? Yep, this is just like hanging out with my family. I'll put a flower on her."

"You just got here," strategy dude said.

"Yeah, and?" Eliza asked.

Helena glanced over at Makoa but he quietly sat and watched the game.

"Chee hoo!" bored woman said. "I win."

Blake collected the flower from Chanel. "Hmm, you both bet, do you want half a flower or do you want to let it ride."

"Let it ride," Helena and Eliza both said.

"I want a rematch," strategy dude said.

"Oh, wait your turn," Chanel said. "I'm up next."

She sat across from bored woman and they started playing.

Helena was starting to feel bad for not learning everyone's names. She was also starting to get tired of standing. She'd been on her feet a lot more than usual. The only open seat was basically the other half of a cushy round thing Makoa sat on. Well, she guessed she was going to sit there. Her stomach churned a little again. But this time it felt lighter, like happy nerves.

Chapter 8

"Mind if I sit?" Helena asked.

"Go ahead," Makoa said. His brain emptied of everything he had been meaning to tell her, to say to her, to explain. He could smell her crisp scent, or thought he could even in the heavily recycled hotel ballroom air. She sat with enough inches between them to make a nun proud. Still, he felt like his every nerve ending was attuned to every place her body was in touching distance of his. Like the cells of his body knew she was near.

They all had mic packs still on, even if he could remember all the carefully craft explanations he had come up with. Plus watching people play konane, it was relaxing, and fun. The mood was good, and maybe he could lean into that.

"You play konane?" he asked.

"I have. But my family gets cutthroat. I often just watch. Don't get cursed as much that way."

"Ah, my sisters were always nice to me. Well, that's not true, they were nice until I started winning easily, then they got mean. But I usually could find enough cousins to play with."

"Did you grow up near all your cousins?"

"Not all of them. Plenty are still back on the islands. But my mom and her sister moved here at the same time. And then my dad's brother did too."

"Wait, you grew up in Vegas?"

"No, we were closer to Reno."

"Oh, okay."

"Where'd you grow up?"

"DC. My parents met in college, and then stayed."

"Oh, I remembered that you were in DC. So you've never lived anywhere else? Oh, that sounded judgy. I didn't mean it like that. Just curious really." And okay, Makoa wanted to know what the chances were she might consider a move to Colorado. Or if he got traded elsewhere. DC had a pro hockey team of course. He had told his agent he was open to anywhere. He obviously would love to play for the Vegas team, so his family could easily come see him. But he hadn't grown up with the Vegas team, so didn't have that much loyalty to the team. He could learn to love any team willing to give him a shot.

"Okay, folks," the production assistant said. "The judges are deliberating. We should be ready to take you all back shortly. Please don't go anywhere. Thanks."

Helena's partner moved over near her feet. "Any chance I could get a head massage?"

Helena looked at them. "I don't know that we are there yet."

"Ah well, it was worth asking. I hate waiting."

"Yeah, it sort of make sense how the contestants get so drunk on some of these shows waiting for judging. It's a lot of waiting."

"What show is that?" Makoa asked.

"Oh, like 'Top Chef' or 'The Bachelor.'"

"Though," Blake said, "It's the housewives or that ship show where they get really trashed."

"Well," Helena said, "the ship show is full of people going on a cruise, so like that makes sense. And if I had to deal with those folks, I'd need a lot of alcohol to get through also."

"So true," Blake said.

Makoa didn't watch a lot of reality, except "Chopped" occasionally. He watched a lot of sitcoms, old and new, he wasn't picky. And of course he did some gaming with his team mates. And listened to a lot of audiobooks. Audiobooks made long bus rides much more bearable.

But reality had never quite been his thing. He wanted to contribute the conversation. Keep showing Helena he was a great person to hang out with. Not a person who ghosted people. Not intentionally at least. But this conversation had moved away from his area of expertise.

"Did you see that one episode," Helena asked, "where the one person kept swearing they knew how to steer, and kept trying to sneak in to do it?"

"Oh gosh, and they were too far off shore to dump him. It was ridiculous."

The production assistant reappeared to count heads and lead them all back into the main ballroom.

They lined up with their partners.

"Okay, if we can have Helena and Blake, Makoa and Eliza, and Ali and Abbey over here."

Lili indicated that the other contestants should stand on the other side of the table the judges were lined up at. "Okay, we'll start with you all first. Helena and Blake, yours was a little short, but what there was of it was good. Your lei still look great. So, good job. If there is a performance element again, consider going a little longer."

Blake and Helena nodded. Makoa noticed they had clasped hands.

"Ali and Abbey, yours was the best hula we saw, so kudos. The 'ukulele paying was spirited, and your lei held up, so good job."

Ali and Abbey hugged each other.

"Makoa and Eliza. You each had two lei, which gave you the second highest number of lei. You also played and danced well. So, great job."

"The six of you are all going to the next round. If you can please move to the side."

Makoa scooched himself next to Helena. "Do you think we'll get dinner next?" he asked softly.

"Ssh, I want to listen to this."

Makoa did not. He was good at tuning things out. His freshman year roommate had been a ginormous snorer. Makoa had learned to start humming inside his mind and tune out what was going on around him. What the judges did or didn't say about a challenge what was over wasn't going to help the next challenge. If he recalled correctly, they had poi, beer, missionaries, and televisions left. So they'd have to see how the judges decided to interpret that.

He was much more interested in finding more ways to spend time with Helena. Preferably without cameras and mic packs, but he wasn't picky.

THEY HAD BEEN GRANTED a dinner break after the judges made the ultimate decision about the remaining pair and now, they were down to eight.

By Helena's count, there were 4 days of Christmas left, but given the way they'd been combining days, probably less challenges. So, they must be planning something to bring the contestant numbers down.

She hugged her tutu.

"Okay, go sit with your new friends," Tutu said. "I can dinner with people my own age."

"I'm in Vegas to hang out with you though."

"And you have. Plus, we'll have more time tomorrow. You hang with your friends. I will go brag you up."

"Okay, Tutu." Helena could tell her tutu really was serious about the bragging which was both sweet and cringey at the same time. So fine, she could eat with a contestant. It would not be Makoa of course, who was currently being hugged up by what looked like his sisters.

But Eliza or Chanel maybe.

Helena grabbed a plate of food first. And then suppressed all the first day of school jitters trying to find someone to sit with brought up, and found a table and sat down next to - oh crud, that was not Chanel she sat next to, it was Makoa's sister. Well, Helena was too hungry to find a new table. Sitting next to him twice in a row was hardly much of a signal. But given how quickly they had hopped into bed last night,

Makoa could be forgiven for considering this a hopeful sign. And who knows, maybe Helena was willing to let bygones be bygones. Or at least wait to hear what his explanation was. Probably not in front of his sister though.

"KAIMANA, THIS IS HELENA," Makoa said.

"I'm Blake," Blake said, sliding into the chair next to her.

"Oh my gosh," Helena, said to Blake, "I feel like I've seen you somewhere before."

Makoa smiled. Watching Helena be silly was a new thing. He liked it.

"Were you the one holding the 'ukulele?" Blake asked.

"Yes, right, you were dancing it's all coming back to me." Helena giggled. She turned to Kaimana. "Sorry, clearly I'm a little punch drunk having been going back and forth between ballrooms all day. Plus, I had an early flight this morning so I am running on a lot of caffeine. But it's nice to meet you."

"Same. Well, I didn't have an early flight. I didn't sleep because my kids love jumping on hotel beds well past their bedtime"

"You let them jump on the hotel beds?" Makoa asked. "Mom and dad let them jump on the hotel beds? Our mom and dad?"

"Well, as grandparents they let the keiki get away with everything. But also, yes, I let my kids jump on hotel beds. Because whatever. They like it. And I hoped it would tire them out. It took longer than expected. But we ran them ragged at the pool today. But, I'm still telling them to wake you up if they need anything tonight."

"Cool," Makoa said.

"How old are your kids?" Blake asked.

"Four and six," Kamana said. "And my sister has one who is three. Just muli hope slacking in the kid department."

"Am I slacking when you all have already populated the next generation?" Makoa asked. Also, you like calling me to be the babysitter."

"Well, that worked better when you were local. Now I can only make you babysit on family vacations."

"When they get a little older you can just ship them to me."

"Please, I've seen your schedule. You're hardly home in season."

"Do you travel a lot for work?" Blake asked.

"He plays hockey," Kaimana said before Makoa could answer. "So he's always on the road for games.

"I get the summer off from traveling at least," Makoa said.

"You should come home with us next week, and stay longer."

"Or, I could sneak the kids in my suitcases."

"I'm told the TSA frowns on that."

"Weird, that's not what you said when you stuffed me into dad's suitcase."

"I know. Must be a new safety rule."

"Oh, I think I heard about that," Blake said.

Makoa raised his eyebrows at Blake. "You're an older sibling, aren't you?"

"Was it my air of responsibility?" Blake asked.

Helena laughed. "Sorry," she said when Blake looked at her. "Yes, air of responsibility, I can see it now."

"Lemme guess," Kaimana said turning her gaze to Helena. "Only child?"

"Yep," Helena said. "Though most people guess I'm an oldest."

"Probably because they are younger kids," Kaimana said. "So, you have nieces, nephews, niblings nearby?"

"Here?" Helena asked. "My Tutu is the only relative who came to the expo."

"In general. Where you live and stuff."

"Kaimana," Makoa said. "She is not one of your interview subjects." He appreciated the info but Helena was started to get that caged look people sometimes got when Kaimana turned her journalistic lens on them. Like they'd been caught under a magnifying glass and wanted to skitter away.

"What, I didn't ask her to describe her policy positions? We're at a Hawaiian Expo. I asked her about her family. It's what we do."

"No niblings nearby," Helena said. "The relatives with kids are mostly on the islands still, so I see them when I'm able to fly there."

"How often is that?"

"Kaimana," Makoa said. "New subject. Do the niblings know konane? Blake got folks playing while we were waiting."

"Oh gosh, I haven't played konane in forever. We'll see if they know how to play a game that isn't on a screen."

"There's an online version too," Blake said. "If that helps."

"It might." Kaimana said. "Though it would be nice if we could get them doing more things not on a screen. Other than jumping on beds. And swimming. But maybe the app and then we can get a board. If we get one now, they'll just end up throwing the pieces at each other, it will be a mess."

"We played with leaves and flowers, so less messy, or I guess, different messy," Blake said.

"Okay contestants," a production assistant shouted. Makoa really should have asked their names by now. "We're going to be back in about five minutes?"

"Have they told us how many challenges left?" Helena asked. "I mean, this is fun and all, but I kind of hoped for a nap or some sunshine today."

"They are doing the closing ceremony in this ballroom tomorrow afternoon, according to the schedule," Kaimana said. "So you should definitely be done before then."

"I asked," Blake said, "but they said they wanted to maintain the surprise."

"Okay then," Helena said. "Let me caffeinate some more. And go hug my tutu. See you guys in there." She waved.

"You are so heart eyes for her," Kaimana said when Helena was barely two steps away.

"And you lack all subtlety."

"So you knew Helena already?" Blake asked.

"Just met her today," he said.

"Muli hope is a jump first, ask questions later kind of person."

"Look," Makoa said, "not all of us found the love of our lives in our math class, okay?"

"True," Kaimana said. "I was smart to lock that down early."

"Okay, people," the PA said. "I need the contestants over here."

Kaimana squeezed Makoa's shoulder. "If you make it to the finals, I'll bring the niblings over to watch. Or take a video for them. Something."

Makoa understood this to be the big sis version of great job, and nodded his thanks. He make a shaka at her, and she shaka'd back.

"You two are making me miss my siblings," Blake said.

"Are they here?" Makoa said.

"Yep. They are gambling though. Not paying any attention to me."

"Ah," Makoa said. As an athlete he generally stayed far away from gambling. People always thought it was weird, that he'd grown up in Nevada and didn't gamble much. But he'd grown up in Nevada, around all these people who worked in casinos. Heard endless stories of great wins and so many more great losses. Plus the line between gambling and sports, was also a dangerous thing to play with, so he figured staying all the way out was safest.

"Well, I hope you get paired up with Helena again. I'm happy to ship it for you."

"Thanks," Makoa said. It was too much to explain he needed more than shipping vibes. Sure she had sat down to eat with them, but it was clear she hadn't realized he was at the table until later. But maybe this next challenge would help him at least seem slightly less terrible to her.

Chapter 9

"Okay, my coconuts, another team challenge," Lili said. "Our papaya tree is back again. You know what to do."

They picked their mynah birds. And this time Helena was paired with Chanel. Makoa got paired with Blake. Which was fine. Chanel seemed very competent. Helena wasn't sad about this pairing. Nope. She was not.

"Coconuts," Lili said, "a word of warning this time. We will do a double elimination again. So two teams are going home. We have made it to our ninth day of Christmas, and I know we are all feeling that Kalikimaka spirit. I'd sprinkle you with tinsel right now, but your next challenge involves food, and we don't want any tinsel in our food."

Helena wanted to make her tutu proud, and okay at this point she wanted to make it to the finals. She definitely should have asked what the days of Christmas were. Guess she was going to find out.

A production assistant wheeled out a large cart. The tablecloth laying over the lumps on top of the table. The production assistant whipped off the tablecloth to reveal taro.

"That's right, my coconuts, we're going to that fabulous staple food, the taro or kalo. And we're going to make poi. Now of course the traditional way involves cooking the taro in an imu for several hours. As cool as that would be, we have some time constraints. And it turns out our lovely hosts here at the Lovestar Hotel do not want us burying ovens on their grounds. I know. Their beds are soft and cozy, but they are a little particular about how guests use their lawns. So, we're doing what Hawaiians have always done and adapting."

Their cooking stations were rolled back out, each topped with a shiny electric pressure cooker.

"Thanks to the very kind people at Fastcook," Lili said, "you each have a pressure cooker. There are also gloves, knives, a mortar and pestle, and a food processor. We are going to give you two and a half hours for this next challenge. Any questions?"

Blake raised his hand. "Any preference for one or two finger poi?"

"Oh, on that I will let you folks surprise me. But that reminds me. We are going to ask each of you to taste your poi before you serve it. Okay. Time starts now!"

Gloves. Helena reached under and put hers on. She didn't usually cook with gloves, but it made sense after the other contestant injured themselves that they'd give them gloves this time. Helena's auntie who was in charge of poi cooking always wore gloves too, because she had a fancy manicure. Helena didn't have much of a manicure right now, but it helped her feel like she was channeling her auntie.

"Have you ever made poi before?" Chanel asked. "Because I have."

"I haven't-" Helena started.

"Okay, you know how to chop, though, right? So chop, small pieces like this big." Chanel picked up one of the taro with her bare hands.

"Here, do you need your gloves?" Helena held out the other pair.

"What am I, a tourist?" Chanel said.

Um, okay. Little rude considering Helena wore the gloves. But whatever. She was not going to take them off now.

Chanel chopped a piece of taro and then held it up for Helena to see. "The pieces should be about this big." She twisted it in her hands, holding it close to Helena's face.

"Got it," Helena said. She had watched poi being made before. She just hadn't been back to Hawai'i as an adult very much. And it was the adults in her family, under Auntie Pika's guidance, who got to make poi. Kids and teens either played, or watched the littler kids play.

She looked at the gloves again. Lili had said they would all have to taste first. Something was itching the back of her brain.

Chanel started chopping in a manner that seemed excessively loud. Helena glanced around, everyone else was chopping and working. And, not that it mattered, everyone else was wearing the gloves.

Helena popped open the pressure cooker. Her tutu had a similar model. Helena loaded some of the pieces she had chopped into the bowl.

"That one's too big," Chanel said. She grabbed a piece out of the cooker and put it on her own chopping board, chopping it in half.

Helena chopped more pieces. She knew even sizes would make the cooking go more smoothly, which was the only reason she wasn't chopping seven different sizes right now.

So Chanel was particular. Maybe she was a chef or something.

"Do you cook a lot?" Helena asked.

"Not if I can help it," Chanel said. "But I am definitely not going down on a simple poi challenge, so here we are."

Chanel turned away and sneezed into her elbow. "This hotel air must be getting to me. I usually don't get allergies or anything."

Helena finished chopping another taro and tossed the pieces into the pot. Chanel sneezed into her elbow again.

A PA moved over to them. "Have you two made poi before?" he asked, holding up the camera.

"I've made poi multiple times. Helena here is a newbie though."

"I've watched it made though. And I am also very good at eating it," Helena said. It was mostly true. She liked poi. But it was something she had when it had been made by friends or family, and almost never missed when it wasn't nearby. But if all you needed was a pressure cooker and some time, maybe she should change that. Her family didn't use an imu to make poi. They went with the boil it down method which took a while, and created a lot of humidity. Hawai'i didn't have a lot of humidity, unless it was voggy season. But DC had quite a bit. So the idea of sitting while everything boiled had seemed awful.

But a pressure cooker would mean she could chop and then go do much more interesting things while the taro cooked. Then running things through a masher or food processor and she'd have poi. Huh. Helena wondered if Auntie Pika would go for that.

"Why did you decide to skip the gloves?" the PA asked.

"Oh, I don't need gloves to cook poi. I'm Hawaiian," Chanel said.

Helena wanted to point out that everyone currently wearing gloves was Hawaiian too, but that seemed like not good team behavior even if Chanel had started it.

"Lots of people are afraid of taro or confuse it with ube," Chanel said. "It's actually completely different. And very delicious."

Helena looked over and watched as Chanel tossed a small piece in her mouth.

"No!" Helena said. Because now she remembered what had been bugging her. "Medic!" she yelled.

"Did you cut yourself?" Chanel asked.

Helena reached for Chanel's hands and pulled them away from the taro. Chanel's hands had small red bumps on them. "The gloves were because of the chemical in raw taro."

"Calcium oxalate," the woman in scrubs said. "Did you eat any?"

"She ate a small piece," Helena said.

"Does your throat hurt?" the medic asked.

"A little," Chanel said.

"Okay, I'm going to take you over to the side and see if we can get you with a little milk to help or if we need to give you some antihistamines."

Helena kept chopping. "Don't worry, Chanel, I'll keep going."

"Okay, but don't overcook the taro," Chanel said. "And don't put too much water in it. No one likes four finger poi."

Helena nodded.

"You doing okay?" Makoa asked.

"Don't you have your own poi to worry about?" Helena asked. It was sweet of him to have come over to her station, but she was fine. She was wearing gloves.

"We're fine."

"Are you sure Blake feels that way?" she asked. "Go help your teammate. I'm fine."

Helena finished chopping the taro, and got it all in the pressure cooker. She added a little water to help it all steam, and set it for 90 minutes. And now they waited. She could go over and check on Chanel, but well, Chanel seemed fine.

She looked up and spotted her tutu in the crowd and gave her a smile.

Looking around, one of the teams was still chopping, but the rest were all staring at their pressure cookers.

Helena was used to being able to scroll her phone while she waited. Maybe she felt a teeny bit bad about shooing Makoa away. But given how many people in this ballroom were staring at their pressure cookers, did she want to give the folks watching upstairs an extra show? Helena glanced over at Makoa quickly, noting the dark blue shirt he was now wearing. Yeah, she might be up for creating a little more drama.

MAKOA HEARD THE CALL for a medic and froze. Fortunately, the knife in his hand had frozen too or he would have needed the medic himself. Was Helena okay? Was she hurt, injured, unwell?

He watched as Helena talked to the medic and the medic turned and looked at Chanel. After few moments, the medic led Chanel away and Helena went back to chopping.

Makoa felt some of the worry drain out of him. He felt a little bad to be relieved that Chanel was hurt, though he hadn't seen any blood.

Chanel seemed okay over in the corner with the medic. Alert and upright at least.

Makoa checked in with Helena, but she shooed him back to his team. Makoa had returned and finished chopping the taro. Now he and Blake had everything in the pressure cooker and they were waiting. Blake had wanted to do 60 minutes, Makoa was sure they needed 90, so they compromised on 75.

"Dude," Blake said, "if I may call you dude. We're just staring at our pressure cookers. Go talk to her."

"You may call me dude. I sports. Dude is fine."

"You sports. I feel like - wait no - pin." Blake mimed moving something to another column.

Impressive mime. Makoa had played with people who thought a raised eyebrow while wearing a hockey shield was great communication. Admittedly, on the ice sometimes that was all you had time for before the other team noticed.

"Go, talk to her. We'll talk sports later," Blake said.

And Makoa liked being a good team member, so he did.

Except, as he stood near Helena, he realized the problem was he didn't know what to say exactly. Hi, Helena, please forgive me for not coming back to give you more orgasms was not something he thought he should say while miced up.

And he didn't know what the weather was like outside this ballroom. So, he kind of was left with not much. "Hey, how's it going?" he asked.

"I'm doing okay. Just letting the pressure cooker do its thing. I'm fine. You can go back to your teammate."

"He sent me here," Makoa said.

"Oh my gosh," Helena said. She waved hi over at Blake. "I really am capable of watching a pressure cooker all by myself.

"I know," Makoa said. "I just figured, since we're waiting, we could chat or something."

Helena tapped her collarbone near where her mic was attached. "You thought we could chat now?"

"Well, do you have other plans at the moment?" he asked.

"No, fair point. So, what did you want to talk about?" she asked.

He was sure at some point he had struck up a conversation with someone before. what had they talked about? How had he ever talked to her in a bar? "Well, what's your plan for tomorrow?"

"It kind of depends on if we end up here all night. But I heard the pool is gorgeous, so I definitely want to check that out."

"My niblings went to the pool. Kaimana said they all had fun."

"You are always very good about calling them niblings."

"Well, it makes more sense, right? Like it isn't gendered. It's weird the things we gender in language."

"Oh you are not kidding. I took French in high school and table is gendered. Like why does the table need a gender? Not saying tables can't have genders. Just saying, getting dinged on my French test because I couldn't remember the gender of table was annoying."

"Fair. I took Spanish. Though if I'd been planning ahead, Swedish would have been so smart."

"More hockey players from Sweden than Mexico, I'm guessing?"

"Yup." He smiled. He liked how quickly she caught on to that.

"Have you always played?"

"Pretty much. One of the summer camps I was in as a kid did an ice day, and I was hooked."

"Oh wow. And as the muli hope I guess they were okay with team sports."

"You sound like someone who has some familiarity with team sports life."

"No. Well, not any more. I was briefly, a swimmer. But they had to redo the pool the following year. The team moved to another location, and my parents were like look, if you want, we can figure this out. But you have to be committed to swim life, and if you're not, then take a year off and you can always go back the next year."

"You took a year off?"

"I took the rest of my life off. I liked swimming. I even liked swimming competitively. But I also liked hanging out with my friends, and not doing my homework on a bus. And I was good, but not great. Sure, maybe that would have changed with more practice. But I felt like the fact that I didn't care that much meant I was not going to be the next Katie Ledecky. I'm not like sad about it."

"Well, now I really do want to see you get some pool time."

Helena gave him a sly look. "You should have always wanted to see me in a pool."

Makoa cleared his throat. Gosh this hotel air was dry, and he was in a ballroom with goodness knows how many family members watching him, to say nothing of the cameras everywhere. "I did," he said, "always want to see you in a pool. Now I just want it more. For you." And him too. But that was off mic talk.

HELENA WAS ENJOYING Makoa too much for someone she had sworn not to, well, enjoy anymore. She watched the readout on the pressure cooker. And okay, clearly she owed Blake and their shipping ways.

Chanel seemed fine, still over in the corner with the medic. She had lost that determined focused edge, which likely meant they had dosed her with some antihistamines and she was out for the count.

Helena and Makoa were still chatting when she heard the chime of one team's pressure cooker go off. She glanced at her pressure cooker, but it still had twenty minutes left.

"Oh that's much too soon," Makoa said. "Unless they didn't use all their taro."

Helena had kind of picked a time based on the time left, more than anything else. She didn't have a pressure cooker at home. But she also had been in charge of mashing potatoes enough times to know you could almost never be too soft, but you could definitely be too hard. In potatoes, that is. Not so much in other things.

Oh goodness. Helena had a pretty high sex drive, but here Makoa had her thinking about sex in regards to potatoes. Although, well, potatoes were very sexily delicious. So maybe that was less Makoa and more the potatoes. And maybe she was little punch drunk from having been stuck in this ballroom all day with not enough sleep or rest.

But all her mad at Makoa seemed to have fizzled away.

Helena watched the two contestants load their taro into the food processor. They pressed the button to whirl the blades and the top flew off. Helena stilled her face so she didn't chuckle. Makoa grabbed her hand and squeezed it. When she looked at him, she detected a hint of mirth in his eyes but his face was otherwise expressionless.

When had she learned what his eyes looked like when he tried not to laugh? How had she learned so much about him in so little time?

The two contestants, David and Ali, that was their names, started scooping up the taro that had splattered. David held it over the food processor and Helena winced, because no, do not put that back in there. Ali pulled the food processor away and they had what looked like an intense conversation before David waved over a production assistant.

Eliza and Abbey's pressure cooker chimed and a few minutes later Blake and Makoa's chimed.

"Go back to your teammate. I'll be fine," Helena said.

Makoa walked back over. Helena thought about breaking into her pressure cooker, but wasn't sure how to do that without getting burned so decided to lean into it. Figuratively and not, as a camera person came over to her and asked, "Are you worried you left your taro in there too long?"

"I'm not worried that I left it in there too long," she said, including the question in her answer as they had been instructed. "It will be much easier to prep it, due to the extra cooking time."

She hoped it was true. But she had mashed a bunch of potatoes with a plain old dinner fork once when she agreed to be the mashed potato person for a Friendsgiving. A food processor and a pestle, this should be easy. A plan for her and Makoa and a pool not surrounded by cameras or an audience, that was hard. But Helena was very good at logistics. Especially the logistics that involved hot people.

Chapter 10

Helena's arm was going to fall off. She glanced at the clock again. Six minutes left. This was both great and terrible news. She was not done. She was not sure she would be done in six minutes. But, in six minutes she would have to stop. So, okay. She pulled out the bowls they had been given for serving and started arranging some of the stuff she had mashed already, putting some in each bowl. And then she resumed mashing.

"Hey, can I help?" Makoa asked.

Helena glanced over. Blake was still whirling taro in the word processor. "Help your teammate first."

"He said it was fine."

"Makoa, I'm fine. Help your teammate."

"Are you sure?"

"The offer is appreciated. Help your teammate."

When a production assistant announced the final minute, Helena moved the last of the taro in to the bowl. She stirred it a little to disguise a clump that she could see. At time she raised her hands in the air to indicate she was no longer touching anything.

She looked around. Most everyone looked a little tired. The long day was starting to get to everyone.

A production assistant had them each take a taste of their poi. Helena thought it was pretty good. There was a tiny clump, but hopefully that was the last one.

Lili came around and tried some of everyone's poi, noting texture, thickness and flavor. The contestants were gathered, along with Chanel, to stand in front of Lili's stair podium.

Lili looked down at them. "Okay, before we get the cameras back on, I want to say you all have been wonderful. We are almost done for tonight. And then some of you will be returning tomorrow. Okay, cameras are on. Hello, my coconuts. Well, we've made it through to 9 pounds of poi, as our song advises us of our Christmas presents. Between you, you had about 9 pounds of taro to transform into poi, with the help of your Fastcookers. There were challenges, some of you learned firsthand why we have to handle raw taro carefully. And some of you learned not to rush the process. We're island people at heart. Things that need time to properly cook are things we love to eat."

Lili did a little shimmy. "Okay, let's start with some good news. Makoa and Blake, you two made my favorite poi. Good two finger thickness. Good texture. And we saw you two working well together and also offering assistance to a fellow teammate. So, great job, you are through to the finals."

Makoa and Blake high-fived.

"Ali and David, your poi ended up runny and chunky which was not a great combination. I'm sorry to say this is the last day of Christmas for you."

"Abbey and Eliza, your poi had a good thickness but was a little grainy. So, this will also be your last day of Christmas."

"Yay!" Chanel said.

Helena glanced at her. Celebrating early wasn't just tacky, it was unwise. Lili might be planning to eliminate everyone who wasn't Makoa or Blake. But Chanel was probably still foggy from the antihistamines.

"So, that leaves us with Chanel and Helena. I confess, I struggled. The poi you produced was good, but it was very clear that was as a result of only one part of the team."

"But I had a medical issue," Chanel said.

"You did have a medical issue, but it was self-inflicted." Lili gave her a serious, you are on notice look. "But I decided in the spirit of

Christmas to let you go forward. But just know, I expect you to be amazing in the finals."

Chanel nodded.

"So, Helena, Blake, Makoa, and Chanel, we will see you in the finals. Our last day of Christmas will have a lot of spirit. Both aloha and Christmas. Be ready."

THEY'D BEEN GIVEN A call time and instructions for making it to the final event. And finally, they got to leave the ballroom. Makoa immediately followed Helena closely. "Hey, can we talk?"

"Makoa, I need to check with my tutu, and probably get some sleep."

"Breakfast tomorrow?"

"Sure, we can meet at 7," Helena said.

He wanted to hug her, or well, more, but it didn't seem like they were quite there yet. Helena hugged her tutu.

Makoa looked around for his mom or sister. He found his dad.

"Hey, Dad." They hugged.

"Hey, Muli Hope. Looks like you've been having fun today."

"It's been interesting for sure. Did you all get dinner already?" Makoa had eaten, but he knew sometimes his dad forgot.

"I ate at senior citizen time with the niblings. Did they let you take the poi?"

"I didn't ask," Makoa said. "But probably they won't throw it away." He should have thought to ask the production assistants.

"No worries, Muli Hope. We will put you in charge of poi making next time you visit."

"Deal," Makoa said. As the muli hope, he got put in charge of so little of the food. Chopping veggies, sure. But Kaimana was always in charge of dessert. His mom was usually in charge of the sides, his dad whatever meat dishes they had, and his other sister 'Alohi usually made a fruit salad. It was already too much food. No one wanted to relinquish their role or share it with him, so he usually was tasked with of helping his sister's spouses wrangle the niblings. He loved hanging with the niblings, but he cooked at home all the time. He needed to eat, and needed the right balance of protein and carbs to help with stamina and muscle retention, so he couldn't rely too much on packaged food. And yet, he was the muli hope. The roles had already been assigned.

"It was very good of you," Dad said as they approached the elevator bank and stood with cluster of folks waiting for the elevators, "to check on your teammate. Well, I guess technically she wasn't your teammate for that challenge. But you had worked with her earlier? I think someone near me said that."

"Yeah, I had worked with her earlier," Makoa said. It was more than that. Makoa was no longer miced up, but they were surrounded by people who were glancing at him as they waited, so he held off on explaining. Makoa searched the crowd, but didn't see Helena or her tutu. He hadn't thought to get her contact info. Ugh. Or her room number. He didn't even know if the room was under her name or her tutu's.

"Well," his dad said. "You've got your room card, right?"

Makoa nodded, patting his pocket where he had stashed it.

"You should check on her one more time."

Makoa looked around confused.

His dad yelled, "Coming through!" And then pushed a hand on Makoa's back. The crowd parted and his dad pushed him one more time into the open elevator. The doors closed between them and Makoa turned to apologize for his pushy dad and saw that standing in front of the crowd was Helena and her tutu.

"My dad is not usually so..." he trailed off.

Helena's tutu smiled. "I'm sure he was worried after your long day, you might need to decompress."

Makoa looked at all the numbers lit up on the elevator and realized he couldn't remember what floor the room was on. He waited until they got to a floor that Helena and her tutu got off at, and followed. "Are you on the same floor?" Tutu asked.

"So, funny story," Makoa said as the elevator doors closed behind him. "I'm terrible at remembering hotel floor numbers. Or room numbers. So I actually need to text my family and ask, because there's nothing on the key card." He held up the key card that had the Lovestar Hotel logo and nothing else.

"Well, why don't you come to our room and at least you can sit down for a bit while you wait for them to text you back."

Helena gave her tutu a look but nodded. "Come with us."

Their room had a small sitting area and two beds. Tutu poured Makoa a glass of water, and then said she needed a shower, and went into the bathroom and shut the door.

Makoa texted his mom. His dad hardly ever checked his phone, and his sisters would tease him endlessly, but hopefully his mom wouldn't tell everyone. Oh who was he kidding. His mom was probably going to tell one of his sisters to text him.

"So, is now a terrible time to ask for our phone number? Or offer you mine?" Makoa said.

"Oh, sure," Helena said. And she rattled off hers, and he got it entered, and even got her to pose for a picture he added to the contact. Makoa was pretty happy with that. He would have to thank his dad later.

His mom still hadn't texted back.

"So," he said trying to remember how to make small talk with someone who seemed to have forgiven you for accidentally ghosting them. "What do you think they'll have us do tomorrow?"

"Oh, I meant to look up the song." Helena tapped on her phone.

The song began playing. He leaned in closer, though he could already hear. It gave him an excuse to press a little further into Helena on this small hotel loveseat. He didn't think they were going to have a repeat of - wow, had it only been the night before. But he would take this now, leaning against her, while a Christmas song played.

HELENA KNEW HER TUTU was trying to nudge her by giving her alone time with Makoa. It was nice, sitting here listening to a Christmas song. It was still July outside, but somehow having the spent the day in a ballroom filled with twinkle lights, she had decided to embrace the Kalikimaka spirit.

"So, we still have beer, missionaries, and televisions?" Helena said. "I'm almost afraid to think about what they will be having us do tomorrow. Maybe I should have eaten raw taro."

"No, it actually can feel like you are eating glass. Zero out of ten. Do not recommend."

"So, you've done it?"

"I was a little kid. Someone said don't touch or eat the raw taro, and so I did. Learned a lesson for sure that day."

"Oh wow, were you okay? I mean obviously, you are still here. But like did you have to go to the ER?"

"Nah, they gave me some milk, and some kid's antihistamines and I took a long nap, and was fine."

"Oh, well, that's good. So you're saying I should be sympathetic to Chanel. Because the production assistant was in the middle of asking her why she didn't want to wear the gloves when she decided to level up and eat some on camera."

"Oh, so the production assistant set her up?"

"Honestly, I don't think he meant to. I mean, she'd have been itchy if she just went without the gloves. Since they gave us gloves, I think he figured she'd be itchy and they'd have a good example. Not that she'd go one step further."

"Oh, well, then I wouldn't feel that bad. I mean I've been on a bus full of teenagers, and have seen some truly incredible dares go down, but that doesn't sound like what was happening. And even if she hadn't been aware of why we don't eat raw taro, it seems like she was being foolish. Though I guess that's why she survived even though she wasn't much help. Like they probably should have been clearer. No one would have died or anything, but the challenge would have been very boring if everyone ended up needing the medic."

"True. Okay, well, I'm just going to hope if we have more teams, I'm not on her team."

"Fair."

Helena could still hear the shower going. Her water saving tutu seemed to have abandoned all principles tonight. Helena thought back to what Makoa had said about room numbers. And okay, she had sworn not to ask. But now she was actually going to ask. "You forgot my room number, is that what happened?"

Makoa dipped his chin down embarrassed. "Yeah. And I didn't want to knock on like every door because it was the middle of the night, and that's rude, and also I am a big brown dude."

Helena nodded. Yeah, that actually made a lot of sense. And she often didn't exchange phone numbers with people she hooked up with. It made it easier to never see them again if that's what she decided needed to happen.

"I tried to ask the desk clerk, but she wouldn't call anyone in the middle of the night, and also would not give me the room number. All of which was fair, I could have been anyone. But it made solving the problem tricky."

"I can see that. And your family's room. Is your mom not going to text you back?"

Makoa looked at his phone. "Yeah, I figured she might take a while. But, ugh, maybe 'Alohi will take pity on me."

"You know what?" Helena said feeling a surge of energy, restlessness. She had barely sat all day and yet, she could tell, she wasn't going to be able to sleep. The room was too small for her to pace, plus eventually her tutu was going to want to sleep. Probably soon, given the hour. Her tutu usually went to bed around 8, and it was nearly 9. "We never got to go to the pool. Let's do that."

She got up and knocked on the bathroom door. "Tutu? Makoa and I are going to go to the pool for a bit. Need anything?"

"I'm all set," Tutu said, her voice sounding suspiciously close to the door. "Don't worry about waking me up, I can sleep through just about anything."

That was not entirely true, but Helena got the hint. "I won't be out too long. Need my beauty sleep for tomorrow. But I'll be quiet when I get back." She grabbed Makoa's arm and they managed to squeeze carefully around the hotel room door together. "Also, we can stop at the desk downstairs and get your room number."

"Ah, right," Makoa said. Makoa would have thought of that, sooner or later.

Chapter 11

The hotel didn't have a super fancy pool, just a small one, with large signs about a lack of lifeguard, and how swimming was at your own risk. They sat along the edge of the pool. Makoa had gotten the room number from the front desk after showing them his ID. His family still hadn't texted him back but maybe with the niblings asleep, everyone had their phones on silent.

Helena dipped her toes in. "Ah," she said.

Makoa dipped his in. "It's tepid."

"Yeah," Helena said, "I was worried it was going to be cold, since it does not look like it's heated. But this is nice. Not hot, but not freezing. We've been in a highly air-conditioned ballroom for most of the day."

"I'm used to cold," Makoa said.

"Makes sense," Helena said. "I like heat."

Makoa leaned closer. "Oh do you?" he asked. He kissed her, a soft kiss.

Helena pulled back. "Can I ask you a question, no judgement?

"Oh, that's not ominous. But sure."

"Are you wearing the same pants or do you have like three pairs of the same pants?"

"Oh yeah, so funny story," Makoa chucked. "The airline temporarily misplaced my bag. So I got the cab driver to take me to a shopping center where I could buy some shirts. Because the kid next to me on the airplane spilled juice on me."

"Oh wow, you had quite the morning before you even got here."

"Yeah. I probably should have checked in with the airline about my bag. Tomorrow, I guess." He looked at his phone, but calling the airline was not what he wanted to do right now. He finally had Helena to himself.

"You should get your sister to call. You'll be busy in the final challenge."

"True." He wasn't sure either of his sisters would do it. Well, they would. It was more what he would owe them for doing it. "So, I want you to know, I was bummed I couldn't get back to your room this morning - wow, that was just this morning?"

"I know, it feels like days ago."

"But it wasn't just because I wanted to watch you come again, I like you. I wanted to talk with you and get your phone number so we could talk even after this weekend."

"Well, I confess, I was looking forward to you making me come again also. But it does seem that - room number forgetfulness aside - you are an interesting person and I have liked hanging out with you, doing Christmas challenges."

"So, when is your flight back to DC?"

"Monday morning."

"So, I know you need some time with your grandmother too, but somewhere in there, after the challenges, could we hang out some more?"

"We're hanging out right now," Helena said.

"I know, but I want to book time with you now. Also, I figure in a few seconds we will stop talking."

"Oh really," Helena wiggled a little closer. "What's happening in a few seconds?"

He leaned in a kissed her again. He slid an arm around her back, pulling her closer, he ran his other hand along her arm, felling the texture of her skin.

"Hey!" a voice called.

They turned. A hotel employee stood there glaring. "No sex in the pool!"

"We weren't having sex," Makoa said reasonably.

"Yeah, yeah, yeah," the hotel employee said. "You've got rooms right? Use those." He stood there, arms crossed, clearly expecting them to leave.

"Well," Helena said as she moved away and stood up. "I know Tutu said she sleeps through anything, but I don't actually think that's true. I assume your family's room has sleeping niblings in it?"

"Yeah, probably."

"Well, let's go to the bar. We can talk there a bit. Unless you need your beauty sleep for the challenge."

"I am already beautiful," Makoa said.

"True," Helena kissed him quickly. "One drink and then I do need beauty sleep so I can kick your butt tomorrow."

"I look forward to it. Also, we're on for breakfast, right?"

"You are just filling up my dance card, sir," Helena said.

"Yeah, gotta schedule the important things," he said.

They walked past the hotel employee who still had his arms folded. Helena waved.

Once they were seated in the bar, Helena said, "Here's what I think."

Makoa steeled himself, that sounded like a concerning opening.

"I think it's too much, with the show, with us technically competing against each other. I don't think we can reasonably make any decisions about each other or any relationship status until the show is done. So let's hold off on that until tomorrow. After all if I beat you, you might be too butthurt or something."

"I'm an athlete," Makoa said. "I am accustomed to both winning and losing. Really, the concern is what happens if I win. Or Blake wins. Or Chanel?"

"Well, anyway, I think we can manage to table all of that until after the show."

"So we can talk about other things, just not us."

"Correct."

"Okay, so dinner tomorrow?"

"How about breakfast Monday."

"I'll take it." He leaned across and kissed her.

They chatted about other things while they finished their drinks. They kissed a few more times, on their way to the hotel elevator. And inside the elevator until Helena pulled away. "There are cameras in the elevators here." She tugged her dress back down.

He walked her to her room, and kissed her one more time before heading back to his family's room. He looked forward to the competition tomorrow. But he was looking forward to breakfast Monday even more.

Makoa meant what he said. His off-ice plans sometime fell apart, but it just meant he made more. He was going to make as much room for Helena in his schedule as he could. Sometimes his plans fell apart, but he was used to long season, many attempts. Not just here, but after Vegas.

Chapter 12

The niblings awoke at six, which pretty much put the end to Makoa trying to sneak out of the hotel room without his family noticing.

"I'm just going down to meet one of the contestants for breakfast," he said.

There were a bunch of knowing looks.

"Your niblings haven't gotten a chance to eat a meal with you. You should take them with you," Kaimana said.

Makoa glanced over at Marley hoping maybe his sibling-in-law would jump in and protest, but Marley just smiled at him. Makoa was going to remember this. But sure, he could take the niblings, or triple K, since their names were Kainoa, Kalani, and Kaleo with him.

He texted Helena to let her know he was on his way, with three extra guests.

The kids were pretty good getting plates and getting settled in with juice. Kaleo had taken like seven blueberry muffins, but if his siblings worried about a balanced breakfast, they should have come down themselves.

Helena found them and joined with a hefty plate of her own.

"This is my friend Helena," Makoa said. "Helena this is Kainoa, Kalani, and Kaleo."

"Oh, fans of K names I see."

"All the good names in Hawaiian start with K," Kainoa said.

"Kainoa," Makoa said, "We've talked about this."

"It's just the truth," Kainoa said. "Your name's nice too though, But it's not Hawaiian."

Helena leaned closer. "Wanna know a secret?"

All three kids turned towards her.

"My middle name is Hawaiian," Helena said.

Kainoa looked back at their plate, clearly unimpressed.

"What is it?" Kalani asked. Kalani shifted onto her knees on her chair. She often did that to seem taller she said. She was determined to be a basketball player, and said she needed to practice being tall.

"Alaka'i," Helena said.

"Still not a k name," Kainoa muttered.

Makoa thought about reminding Kainoa to be polite, but he knew Kainoa wasn't meaning to be rude. Kainoa was just a big fan of k names. Well, Hawaiian K names.

"What does it mean?" Kalani asked.

"It means leader," Helena said.

"That's a good name," Kalani said.

"Agreed," Makoa said, realizing he'd been letting the niblings do all the work of talking to Helena.

"So," Helena said. "What are you all going to do today?"

"Makoa has to go be on TV again," Kalani said.

"I know, I have to do that too," Helena said.

"Oh. Well, I think we're going to a museum about lights. But then we're going to go to the pool too. Oh, and the market. The market is in here."

"The pool is nice. I went there last night," Helena said with a smile in his direction.

"But Makoa doesn't have a swimsuit. Makoa," Kainoa said. "You are not supposed to wear your street clothes in the pool."

"True," Makoa said. "We didn't go in the pool. Well, we stuck our toes in. But we didn't swim."

He had hoped to get a little kissing in this morning since they had agreed to not talk about their relationship - such as it was - on the show. So far, taro questions, aside, the production assistants had seemed uninterested in creating drama outside of the challenges. But they didn't need to offer up a showmance on a silver platter. So they were going to stick to they met yesterday, which was true-ish, and not provide any additional details. It wasn't a dating show after all.

So maybe the niblings provided a good reminder of how things needed to be until the show completed.

"So do you all remember the song about the twelve days of Christmas Hawaiian style?" Makoa asked.

Kainoa began singing and soon all three niblings were singing the song. When the table next to them joined in Makoa looked at Helena and saw that she was singing too. He joined in, as did another table in the buffet area. They made it through the whole thing.

"Harold," said one tourist in matching floral top, and shorts, along with a green visor, "why are people singing Christmas songs in July?"

"No idea honey, but it sure is catchy," the man next to her said.

"So," Makoa said. "Everything we've been doing on the show is related to the song."

"So, you've been singing Christmas songs all day?" Kainoa asked.

"I love Christmas songs," Kalani said. "Can I come sing?"

"Me too," Kaleo said.

"We haven't been singing much," Helena said. "But like the part of the song about getting coconuts as a gift, so they gave us coconuts to smash open."

"Coconuts are easy to open. You just have to find the eyes," Kainoa said.

"Yep, finding the eyes helps a lot. You're very good at this. Will you do me a favor?" Helena asked.

"I can do it," Kalani said.

"I actually was wondering if all three of you could do it. When you go to the light museum will you make sure to remember your favorite sign there and come back and tell me about it?"

"You should come with us!" Kalani said.

"She has to do the show," Kainoa said.

"Oh, I forgot," Kalani said. "I promise to tell you about my favorite."

"Me too," Kaleo said.

"Of course, I will," Kainoa said. "That's easy."

"Thanks, I appreciate it," Helena said.

Makoa reached over and squeezed her hand. She was great with the niblings. She had been great in each of the challenges. He definitely wished he could kiss her but for now he would squeeze her hand. She squeezed back.

HELENA HAD NOT KNOWN what to expect from breakfast with Makoa, but his niblings tagging along had turned out to be interesting.

He was kind with them and they were clearly comfortable with him. One of Makoa's brothers-in-law had come to collect the kids. And ruffle Makoa's hair. And now she and Makoa were on their way to the ballroom.

They were taken to a smaller conference room to get ready.

She smiled at Blake and Chanel as they all got miced up and reminded of the rules.

After what felt like forever, but according to the clock on the wall was only twenty minutes, they were herded into the main ballroom. There were no carts. The palm trees with twinkle lights were there, along with Lili's stair podium. On one side of the ballroom sat a large collection of tube televisions. It almost looked like a television graveyard.

Next to it was a set of large plastic laundry baskets, each filled to the brim with beer cans. Helena counted. Four baskets. So maybe no teams for this final challenge.

Looking up she could see the upper area was packed. Someone waved but she couldn't tell who it was. She waved back.

"Okay," a PA said. "Once Lili is here, please don't look up at the audience. We just need to finish setting up, and then Lili will be out."

They heard a giant metal screech from the next room. The PA winced and Helena started to feel the excitement, the anticipation zip through her. She had come into this competition wanting to not go out last. And now, while she mostly liked - to degrees varying from didn't hate to absolutely wanted to bang again - everyone left in the competition, she also wanted to beat them. This show might never air. She might have to create a Wikipedia page for it her own self, so she could document her success. But she wanted it now.

Lili came out in a fabulous outfit, complete with red and white floral skirt, green leaf lei on each of her wrists. A white faux fur trimmed crop top revealed amazing abs.

"Aloha, my little coconuts. We have made it to the final challenge for the inaugural season of "The Next Great Hawaiian". She clapped. "And we are down to beer," she held a hand out towards the baskets, missionaries, and televisions."

"You may have noticed we did not bring out the papaya tree today. That's right, my coconuts, you will not be teaming up today. Well, at least not with each other."

The camera people moved in close to catch their reactions.

"So, each of you will need to create an installment, an art piece if you will, using at least ten cans of beer, and at least one television, though no more than twelve. And to assist you in your endeavors, we have some audience members that have agreed to help in the next room over. You need to recruit one, that's the missionary part," Lili winked. "Now, to make things a little more difficult, some of the audience members are actually friends or family members of other contestants. If you request their assistance, they will hand you a heart, letting you know that they cannot assist. Also, if it's your family member they are going to do the same thing, so don't try asking your brother."

Chanel chuckled loudly.

"I've also recruited some judges, to help me, but we are going to save that as a surprise. But one thing to note, we are going to factor in how many beer cans and televisions you use - so points in favor. And how many hearts you collected, points against. They won't be the only things we consider, but keep that in mind."

Lili looked thoughtful.

"Oh right, one more thing. In your installation, none of the beer cans can touch the floor." Lilli winked. "Any questions?"

Chanel raised her hand.

"Do some people have lots of family members in the crowd? Because that seems unfair for them to know more people?"

"We have factored that into the points," Lili said.

Helena was very curious what that meant. She wasn't the least bit artsy, but she was already thinking about how to array the cans on the television. Maybe two, for balance.

Blake held up a hand. "Are we allowed to use glue or any other supplies in the installation?"

"Oh, I am so glad you asked. The people in the stands, each of them has something you may choose to use. They all have different things, and they are not allowed to tell you ahead of time. Anything else?"

Makoa put up his hand.

Helena was starting to feel bad that she didn't have a question. She just wanted to go.

"Do the beer cans need to be empty?" Makoa asked.

"That," Lili said, "is entirely up to you. Any more questions?"

Helena shook her head.

"Alright, my coconuts, you have two hours. Time starts now!"

The big clock started ticking. Chanel, Blake, and Makoa all ran for the adjacent ballroom. Helena moved quickly but was definitely not going to tire herself out. Besides, letting the other contestants hopefully ask some of the wrong people first, would make things easier for her.

Makoa looked back, she waved to show she was fine.

She had a plan, and she was excited. This was going to be a great day.

Chapter 13

The beer tower toppled again and Makoa cursed internally. The person he had eventually recruited had ribbon as their special item, which was adorable, but not very helpful getting beer cans stacked.

"I think we gotta drink them," his helper Zhen said.

"Beer makes me sleepy," Makoa said.

"Then I'll drink them" Zhen said popping one open and chugging.

Makoa had only chugged beer once, at a hockey end of season party. He had felt like dry mouthed death the next day and had vowed to at least enjoy the alcohol he drank from then on.

He looked around the room. Helena's piece was coming together. Her person had had scissors, so they had cut open some of the beer cans.

Blake had an impressive arch of beer cans stretched across two televisions. And Chanel was working with her helper to create what looked like a stack of twelve televisions, each adorned with beer cans.

Makoa understood physics pretty well, you couldn't really play hockey without it. But somehow his ability to visualize was deserting him when it came to these beer cans.

"I'll be back," he said.

Zhen gave a thumbs up.

He looked back over the remaining televisions. He grabbed a cart, and brought over two more, that seemed to have flatter tops. He arranged the beer cans, along them. It wasn't interesting, but. He grabbed the ribbon and decorated the center can atop each TV. That was at least something. He began stacking a few more to make a second layer.

Zhen finished his beer and added it to the stack. "I like it," he said.

"I think this is as good as we're going to get," Makoa said.

"So, you don't need me to drink anymore?'

"No," Makoa said.

"Bummer," Zhen said. "But you're the boss."

The clock counted down the last minutes and a PA yelled time and they all held their hands in the air.

A crash sounded and Makoa looked back, but all his cans were still in place.

Chanel uttered an impressive string of curses before covering her mouth and saying, "Sorry, auntie." Her helper rubbed her shoulder.

The PA's conferred and said something to Chanel that had her shoulders dropping. Makoa made eye contact with Helena and Blake and pointed that they should all go over to Chanel.

"If we all help, then," he shrugged because he wanted to do this. But it seemed unwise to say what can they do to us on a mic that fed exactly to the people who were going to do something.

Blake and Helena nodded and they each moved and started stacking Chanel's beer cans back on the televisions. Chanel joined in. "Thank you all so much."

Two camera operators zoomed in.

They finished and went back to their installations.

Lili came back out.

"Aloha, my coconuts. We are at the final day of Christmas, and I hear there was some extra Kalikimaka spirit in here. We'll talk more about that later. But first, let me introduce you to my judges. I have with me today Nahele, who you may remember from their season on "Project Runway". And Wanaao, who has had art featured in the Honolulu Museum of Art, and the National Museum of the American Indian." The judges each nodded.

"Before we each take a look at the pieces, I understand Chanel's fell down."

"It was fine when they called time," Chanel said.

"And," Lili said, "I understand your contestants all helped you put it back."

"We did," Makoa said.

"What made you decide to do that?" Lili asked.

"Like she said," Makoa said. "It was fine when they called time. And then it fell. We wanted you to get to see it as close to what she intended."

"I see," Lili said inscrutably.

Makoa felt a little like when a teacher was deciding if they were going to punish you or not. Or a coach. Where they said, sure, your overslept, I get it. And then at the end of practice, they'd be like, "Oh, and Makoa's going to sit in goal for a bit while you all practice your shootout. Oh, no need for pads, Makoa, I'm sure your teammates will be able to avoid you."

Lili and the guest judges all came to look at each installation. A PA with a tablet followed, counting up beer cans and televisions.

The contestants were sent back to the other room with the stands the helpers and friends and family had all sat in to wait.

"I think it went well," Zhen said. "Did you think it went well?"

Makoa nodded though he had no idea. He liked winning, but he'd kind of already got the part he cared most about taken care of. Helena had stopped hating him, started kissing him, and he was hoping to maybe spend the rest of the day exploring that. Now he had her phone number at least. He was going to text her, and video chat her, and keep reminding her that he wanted to be part of her life.

They were called back into the ballroom.

"Mele Kalikimaka, my coconuts," Lili said. "I want to thank you all for participating in this inaugural season of 'The Next Great Hawaiian'. First, I will reveal to you our prize. Thanks to the very generous Lovestar hotel, they are offering a penthouse suite for tonight for the lucky winner, along with a dinner from their award-winning chef. The winner will also receive an all-expenses paid weekend at any of the Lovestar hotels worldwide to be used at a later date." Lili clapped.

"Now, first, the extra credits and debits. Chanel had five hearts. She used three televisions, and fourteen beer cans. However, one of our rules was that the beer cans could not touch the ground, and since Chanel's all fell, the beer cans came off the board. We did still factor in the presentation."

Chanel's shoulders slumped.

"Blake, you had three hearts, two televisions, and twelve beer cans. Makoa had two hearts, two televisions, and twenty beer cans. Helena had zero hearts, three televisions, and twenty to beer cans." Lili looked at the guest judges. "Anything you want to say to the contestants?"

Nahele said, "I understand you all have gone through a lot of challenges, and this kind of thing may not have been your wheelhouse. You all created something, and that's great. Blake, I saw what you did, trying to use some crushed cans, and that was interesting. Helena had the advantage of having scissors, but she was the one who transformed the beer cans the most, and that was really fun to see."

Wanaao said, "I agree that seeing people use the beer cans in more interesting ways was nice to see. While only one contestant really transformed things, you all made interesting attempts. These aren't easy items to work with."

"Okay," Lili said. "Thank you so much judges. And we will end the suspense. For your inaugural season of 'The Next Great Hawaiian', our winner, our mea lanakila is Helena Alaka'i Smith!"

Helena gasped and went forward to accept her large shiny envelope with the gift certificate. Makoa applauded. There were cheers from the balcony and a few groans from, Makoa guessed folks who had bet on one of the other contestants.

But he had nothing but happiness for Helena. And he couldn't wait to help her celebrate.

Chapter 14

"Okay, the view up here is pretty cool," Helena said to Tutu. "The Christmas tree is a little weird though."

"Haven't you just won this suite thanks to your Christmas spirit?"

Helena opened her mouth to clarify and then realized she was not going to win that point so it was best to smile and nod.

There was a knock at the door. "If that's more food, tell them I can't do it." Helena remembered herself. "I mean, I'll get it."

Tutu smiled from her spot on the couch.

Helena opened the door to Makoa. "Um, hi. How'd you know where I was?" Helena had texted him pictures of the food, but hadn't sent him the room number.

"I texted him," Tutu said. "I'm going to go back to our room, but I didn't want you to be alone."

"I know what you're doing, Tutu," Helena said.

"Looking after my favorite granddaughter?" Tutu said. "That's right, I am. Now give me a hug."

Helena hugged Tutu, and waved as Tutu blew kisses on her way to the elevator.

She pulled out her phone and texted Tutu to let her know when she made it back to the room.

"So, hopefully I'm a good surprise?" Makoa said.

"Given the decor," Helena gestured to the Christmas tree, "it seems you are a present. A good present. Also, did you eat? Some of it will be cold, but there was so much food. I actually can't believe Tutu didn't take a plate."

"I ate plenty. But we could pack it up - oh, wait, we don't have containers."

"If we get the stuff that needs to be in the fridge, in the fridge, I promise the aunties will have takeout containers. We can let them know tomorrow."

They got everything put away, or wrapped, and stacked up the dishes and such that could go back.

"So," Makoa said. "Now that we are not on camera, not miced up, and not surrounded by my niblings, can we talk?"

Helena made a thinking about it face. "We could, but we could also have sex first?"

"You still have condoms? I actually didn't bring anything with me. But surely in a Las Vegas hotel..."

Helena pulled off her top. She found people often stopped speaking when she did that. Makoa proved the rule. "I have condoms. Did you know this suite has three beds. I think we should start here." She pointed. She unclasped her bra tossing it behind her. She slowed down a little to shimmy out of her pants, and then underwear. She bounced onto the bed fully naked, before remembering she forgot to get condoms.

"Your niblings are right, bouncing on the beds is fun."

Makoa reached for her but Helena held up a finger. "Wait, I forgot condoms."

"Oh, but we don't need those just yet."

She let him tug her back down onto the bed. They kissed. She realized he had gotten naked and she had missed it. She pulled back and stroked his chest, his arms, his sides. He ran fingers across each of her breasts, stroking her nipples.

His hand slid lower and he said, "May I?"

"You should let me get the condoms. Because after you finger bang me, I want you to - well - dick bang me."

"Hmm," he said. "Okay, that sounds like good plan. How far away are these condoms?"

"Not far. You can time me." Helena raced out to the living room and grabbed the condoms from the inner packet in her bag. She separated one packet and tossed the rest. She handed it to Makoa. She stroked her hand back down his front and said, "May I?"

"I want to make you come first."

"I agree to this plan, I just wanted a little touch."

Makoa nodded. She reached down and stroked his cock, watching his eyes, watching the heat build in them as she did, loving the feel of him. She looked forward to more of him, with her, inside her.

He moved her hand. "My turn." He shifted off the bed and moved her so her legs hung partially off the edge. He stroked his hands up the inside of her thighs, leaving trails of heat like arrows. He spread her wide and stroked his fingers across her clit, and then inside her, stroking along her inner walls. his thumb pressed and stroked her clit, and he increased the pressure while speeding the thrust of his fingers. She could feel the orgasm building so fast, it was like she had been waiting forever. It moved up her spine, tightened her thighs and she came, the multicolored lights twinkling across her.

Makoa rolled on the condom and adjusted her legs with her knees bent over his arms. She felt wide open and so, so ready. He slid inside her and they both moaned at the pleasure, the sensation of it all. She swiveled her hips urging him closer, faster, more. And he began to move, thrusting in and against her. Her hands moved down to stroke her clit, and he shifted, his angle changing and she moaned again in pleasure.

She could do this for hours, just like this, with him moving in and out of her, filling her somehow further and deeper, faster and more, waves of pleasure cresting over her.

His tempo changed and she shifted her hips again, moved her hands faster, pressing harder into her clit, and she came again. He shuddered with his own orgasm.

They stilled against each other. Helena felt the cool air waft delicately over them. After a few moments, Makoa grabbed the edge of the condom and pulled carefully out.

"Be right back," he said.

Helena was content to keep laying there. There were lots of decisions she needed to make later. But this was good right now. It might even be something worth trying to hang on to.

"SO," HELENA SAID WHEN Makoa returned from the bathroom, "I rescind what I said earlier."

Makoa froze. "Which thing?" Was she re-thinking things already? He hadn't even had a chance to pitch for an attempt at long distance.

"Yeah, forget fucking in each bed. I vote we just fuck a lot in this bed. We've already broken it in."

"Oh, okay, phew." Makoa sat on the edge of the bed.

"Oh did I worry you?"

"Just a little. But you're fine."

"Well," Helena moved her hands across his chest. "Let's see if I can make it up to you.

Chapter 15

"Helena," Makoa said. "We really should talk." It was quite a few orgasms later. But Makoa knew they needed to do this now before he fell asleep."

Helena rolled to the side which squished her breasts together very distractingly. Somehow, he should be tired. Or not tired, he could not imagine being tired of Helena. But they needed to talk. So he was going to focus on something other than her breasts. "I want us to try this after Vegas. This being us."

"If you're ever in DC and if I'm ever in Colorado?"

"Well, quite honestly, I'm in Colorado now. But I could get traded. And I won't always get first pick of where. But I want us to not like text once in a while, I want us to try a thing."

"I'm going to tell you, I tend more towards short term, no strings stuff. Sex I like. Relationships are hard. Pun not intended. Because if they were the good kind of hard, I would be better at knowing what to do with them. I think that made sense. But we can try video chatting or whatever."

"Okay."

"But I reserve the right to tell you I hate long distance and quit it. It won't be about you, unless you do something stupid again."

Makoa leaned his forehead against hers. "I can't promise I won't do something stupid. But I'm going to try really hard not to. And if we can't make it work, we can't. But somehow I figured the next great Hawaiian wouldn't let a little thing like long distance is hard stop her."

Helena's hand slid down to his butt and pinched.

"Ow," Makoa said.

"I would apologize but you are using my sense of competitiveness against me."

"I am," Makoa said smiling. He kissed her forehead.

"Okay, I apologize because I should not have pinched without permission."

"I forgive you," Makoa said.

"And okay. But you better go make me come again so I have lots of reasons to remember why I agreed to this."

"I like this plan."

"Oh, and Makoa?" she said after he slid deep inside her.

"Yes?" he asked.

"Mele Kalikimaka."

"Mele Kalikimaka."

"And the lights twinkled over them for the rest of the night.

The End

Epilogue

T*he following Christmas (in December this time)* Helena opened her door.

"Mele Kalikimaka," Makoa said.

"Mele Kalikimaka."

They got him and his suitcase inside the door and then Helena shoved him onto the couch and straddled his lap and kissed him. His hands moved under her shirt, resting on the skin along her back where she could feel the warmth spreading through her. Or, she wiggled a little on his lap, maybe it was partly a different kind of warmth.

"Oh, before I forget. Did they tell you they are going to air the show?"

"On the tiny freebie Cassava App? I did hear that. My agent had many thoughts on my violating all his advice for that."

Helena giggled. "Well. Anyway. So. One suitcase. Is that going to last you the rest of the season?"

Makoa had been traded to the minor league team for the Washington Domes, which played in Pennsylvania. But due to an injury he was going to play a few games with the Domes. Helena hoped that would turn into a permanent thing. Because video chat sex was not nearly as good as the real thing.

But also, it turned out that she liked talking with Makoa almost as much as she liked having sex with him. So, being in the same time zone was an improvement, but the same city. Well, it felt like a Christmas present.

"Oh, my tutu wanted a picture of us. We should do it now, since next I want you naked."

"Makes sense," Makoa said.

Helena reached for her phone and took a picture of them, at an angle where the small Christmas tree she'd set up was visible behind them.

She texted it to her tutu.

And then she tossed the phone away. The rest of the relatives could wait. Helena wanted to enjoy her Christmas present.

Acknowledgements

My grandmother's birthday was December 25th, so a couple of our trips to visit relatives overlapped Christmas. And of course, Hawaiian style Christmas songs always featured heavily into our family rotation.

For copyright reasons, I only referenced the song, but I obviously love the song. It is such a fin song, and a reminder that there are people who are making Christmas their own.

Christmas is - for obvious reasons - associated with Christianity. But, many of the things - like trees, twinkle lights, and gathering with loved ones, are found in lots of cultures, and are pre-Christian traditions. In the darkest time of the year (on the northern hemisphere) people looked for coziness and light, even when they do it on a beach. Or in a Las Vegas hotel.

No book gets written alone. The UWS kidlit discord has continued to support me. My fairytale writer friends waited patiently as I wrote this story that demanded it's turn, instead of revising the fairytale. (The fairytale has been revised. Sneak peek available after this.)

And also, thanks to a small clip of a Pacific Islander reality show that I saw years ago, and thought, yeah, that's going in a book someday.

Thanks to my family, both Hawaiian and not. Thanks to my English teachers, who were the first people to tell me I might be good at this writing thing. Thanks to the discords and group chats, where I can go yell that my characters are not behaving and be understood.

And thanks to all my readers. You coming along on this journey with me is a treat.

Reviews are always helpful, so thank you to every reader who tells someone about a book they loved or even didn't. Please consider leaving one on your site of choice.

I love hearing from readers. There's a contact form on my website, a newsletter,and I can often be found on BlueSky these days. Feel free to reach out to me.

Newsletter for info on new releases and what I'm reading and writing can be found here: https://buttondown.email/talkapedia

ARC team signup is here: https://forms.gle/rXz2iqt6VaR8aq6F7

Also by Tara Kennedy

City Complications Series – Adult Contemporary Romance:
Aloha to You –Novella
Undercover Bridesmaid –Novel
Hot Bartender –Novel
City Entanglements Series: Adult Contemporary Romance:
Repeated Burn – Novella
Bored by the Billionaire – Novella
Clear as Ice –Novella
Not an Ending– a bonus epilogue available to newsletter subscribers
Of Kings and Queens - Novella
Too Busy Romance series: Adult Contemporary Romance
Troubled by Love– Novella
Tricked by Love– Novel
Presented with Love – Novella
Standalone Fairy Tale: Romantasy
I Belong to You – Coming Soon
Standalone Short Stories
Bait Girl – A Young Adult Short Story
Called to the Water – An Adult Fantasy Short Story
Dreamcatchers Anthology – A multi-genre, multi-author collection
Non-Fiction:
Let's Talk About Fictional Sex
Find info on where to buy them at www.tarakennedy.com/books[1]

---

1. http://www.tarakennedy.com/books

About the author

Tara Kennedy is a lifelong Washingtonian of Hawaiian, Chinese, and European descent. She wrangles data by day and writes in her spare time. She has dabbled in audio narration. Tara writes romance, but has also had a fantastical short story published in *Commuter Lit*, and in an anthology. Information on books, blog, and newsletter can be found at tarakennedy.com and Tara can also be found on BlueSky as TaraTLK.bsky.social

Preview Chapter

From the upcoming novella: I Belong to You

The three hearts on Makena Kekoa Bauer's bracelet jangled together, and she realized she was fidgeting.

Lo-fi music played while people chattered and put their names down on the list to perform in the open mic night.

Makena's moms had made music a huge part of their life growing up. Even in their other forms, Mama Kahawai's giant lizard, Mom Anna's sleek horse, they laughed, sang,and made music. They were water guardians for Rock Creek, but making time for music had been almost as important as looking after the water.

"Okay, folks, we're going to get started in just a few minutes," a guy in a skinny tie said.

Makena reminded herself, she sang and played 'ukulele all the time. Usually for the trees and birds, but trees were a tougher audience than people knew. Oaks could be real hecklers, especially in fall.

There were no trees or birds inside this coffee shop. She listened carefully. There were a few mice and a salamander.

A salamander. She looked around. *Peri, did you follow me?* she thought.

Duh.You gonna play for the humans?

Yes. Please don't... Makena had so many don't and was pretty sure Peri would laugh off all of them. Don't let the humans see you.Don't cause trouble. Don't.

Since her moms had gone, she had focused on being the best water guardian, on making the line of mo'o and nixies she was descended from proud. And she hadn't been doing anything fun.

Also, she had been a little mad at the humans. They were the ones that made cars, and it was a car that killed her moms.

So,she decided to come play for the humans. She saw humans all the time in Rock Creek Park, of course. Even was friendly with some of the rangers and regular runners. But she needed to remember the good things about humans. Like their love of music. But if a human freaked out over a salamander being indoors, it was kind of going to defeat the purpose. There was a reason she had come in human form and not gecko or dragon. Well, it was also easier to carry a 'ukulele as a human.

Don't worry about me, Peri said.

And with another finger swipe across the heart charms, Makena decided to take that excellent advice.

LEIF SHILLINGFORD KNEW his father would laugh at him for being at an open mic night. Just about everything Leif knew about music he had learned from growing up in tour buses and stadiums watching his father perform.

Leif was back in the DC area for a few weeks, helping his mom with recovery from foot surgery. He would return to his dad's tour where Leif worked as production manager, once she was literally back on her feet.

His mom had practically shoved him out the door tonight. "Please go out," she had said. "Your itchy feet are making me stir crazy."

She always called it itchy feet. The thing that made his dad sign up for tours around the world, even when it finally cracked his marriage. The thing that meant Leif had arranged to do remote school, so that he could finish high school on tour with his dad.

But Leif loved being around live music. He loved the emotions and the surprise.Leif loved live music, even when it sucked. Obviously good live music was preferable. But the possibilities that live music offered were what made it fun. So he figured a night of live music would tame his itchy feet. And then he could go back and be fully present for his mom.

The first dude on stage clearly had big aspirations. His guitar shone in the light,his hair was styled in a way that was meant to look accidental, but its lack of movement betrayed the amount of product. And the t-shirt, jeans, and boots looked stiff and expensive. His voice was good, his guitar work passable, but he didn't have that edge. He sang a song about sadness, while seeming like he had never experienced a sad moment in his life.

The next woman was wonderful, but needed to learn to sing from her diaphragm or she'd blow her voice out, even with today's fancy microphones. The microphone was doing its best, as was the sound guy in back, but she was louder than she was good. She raced off the stage as soon as her song ended.

The next performer carried a 'ukulele and Leif cringed internally. The 'ukulele was a great instrument, it wasn't its fault at all that people tended to associate with only three songs. It was kind of like the bagpipes and "Amazing Grace".

Hmm. Maybe his dad could add a bagpipe to "I Belong to You". It was his dad's most popular song, much to his dad's chagrin, since most of his music was more serious. Story songs about the environment and the working class. But everyone loved a catchy love song. So it got performed in every set, in every venue.They were always looking for ways to change it up.

When the performer strummed the first few chords, Leif sat up straighter. And when she sang a smoky, ethereal, haunting version of Billie Eilish's "Ocean Eyes" he leaned forward. Part of him wanted to get up, walk closer to the stage. Sit at her feet if needed. Only years of good concertgoer etiquette held him back.

She finished and there was a collective pause, that moment when the listeners were all too entranced to move before finally bursting into applause and cheers.Leif applauded. The performer stepped down off the stage. He watched people come talk to her, touch her, congratulate her.

Leif was used to this too. The fans who wanted to gather up a little more of the magic of music, who wanted to talk longer, hold onto the feelings the music had given them.

She seemed to be handling it okay, but he knew plenty of performers seemed fine until they cracked.

The host got up and announced a short break. Leif guessed the next performer wanted a moment before they had to follow that.

He stood and made his way towards her. He hadn't paid attention when the host announced her name.

"Hi,Leif, you made it! So good to see you."

Leif turned and smiled. "Chen! Hey, man, I meant to come say hi." Chen owned the coffee shop, which was how Leif had known they hosted an open mic night.

"How's your mom doing? Is she here tonight?" Chen asked.

"She's doing good. She's resting her foot. Kicked me out of the house though."

"And you decided to come see some music," Chen said. "You picked quite the night."

"Is she a regular?" Leif nodded towards the last performer.

"Never seen her before. Let's go say hi." Chen gave his shoulder a thump and moved towards the performer.

Leif followed.

"Hi,"Chen said, "I'm Chen, the owner of the shop. So nice to meet you." He held out his hand.

The fan who held the performer's hand looked down and dropped their hand, as if they just realized they were still holding onto it. Chen and the performer shook hands.

"I'm Makena," she said, tipping her head, making her long dark hair shift on her shoulders.

"Well, Makena, you sure have some talent there. This is my friend Leif and I'm sure he'd agree, after all his dad is- "

"Not here, today, but my dad also appreciates great music," Leif said quickly. "It really was great."

"Thanks,"Makena said. "Everyone here is so nice."

The host announced they were going to start back up soon, and asked everyone to get seated.

"Come by again, when we can chat," Chen said. "You too, Makena. We'd love to have you back, open mic night, or any other time."

"Thanks,"Makena said.

"I'll text you," Leif said to Chen. Makena's eyes looked a little glazed, like she was reaching the over-stimulation point. "Makena," he leaned in a little closer so he could drop his voice, "did you want to stay or go somewhere a little quieter?"

"Quieter,"she said.

"I know just the place." He led her and her 'ukulele out the door.

Author note: This is a sneak peak from I Belong to You, *a fairytale remix. A group of us decided to remix some Grimm fairytales, and I chose* The Nixie of the Mill Pond, *and of course mixed in a little Hawaiian mythology too. Coming soon, please check the website and/or sign up for the newsletter to be alerted.*

Newsletter here: https://buttondown.email/talkapedia

Website here: www.tarakennedy.com/books[1]

Don't miss out!

Visit the website below and you can sign up to receive emails whenever Tara Kennedy publishes a new book. There's no charge and no obligation.

https://books2read.com/r/B-A-GUVI-AHTCF